EAST JERUSALEM NOIR

EAST JERUSALEM NOIR

EDITED BY
RAWYA JARJOURA BURBARA

*Translated from Arabic by Roger Allen, Marilyn Booth,
Catherine Cobham, Raphael Cormack, Sawad Hussain,
Dr. Nazih Kassis, Nancy Roberts, and Max Weiss*

BROOKLYN, NEW YORK

Published by Akashic Books
©2023 Akashic Books
Copyright to the individual stories is retained by the authors.

Paperback ISBN: 978-1-61775-985-7
Hardcover ISBN: 978-1-63614-088-9
Library of Congress Control Number: 2023933959

Series concept by Tim McLoughlin and Johnny Temple
East Jerusalem map by Sohrab Habibion

Akashic Books
Brooklyn, New York
Instagram, Twitter, Facebook: AkashicBooks
info@akashicbooks.com
www.akashicbooks.com

ALSO IN THE AKASHIC NOIR SERIES

MARSEILLE NOIR (FRANCE), edited by CÉDRIC FABRE

MEMPHIS NOIR, edited by LAUREEN P. CANTWELL
& LEONARD GILL

MEXICO CITY NOIR (MEXICO), edited by PACO I. TAIBO II

MIAMI NOIR, edited by LES STANDIFORD

MIAMI NOIR: THE CLASSICS,
edited by LES STANDIFORD

MILWAUKEE NOIR, edited by TIM HENNESSY

MISSISSIPPI NOIR, edited by TOM FRANKLIN

MONTANA NOIR, edited by JAMES GRADY
& KEIR GRAFF

MONTREAL NOIR (CANADA), edited by JOHN
McFETRIDGE & JACQUES FILIPPI

MOSCOW NOIR (RUSSIA),
edited by NATALIA SMIRNOVA & JULIA GOUMEN

MUMBAI NOIR (INDIA), edited by ALTAF TYREWALA

NAIROBI NOIR (KENYA), edited by PETER KIMANI

NEW HAVEN NOIR, edited by AMY BLOOM

NEW JERSEY NOIR, edited by JOYCE CAROL OATES

NEW ORLEANS NOIR, edited by JULIE SMITH

NEW ORLEANS NOIR: THE CLASSICS,
edited by JULIE SMITH

OAKLAND NOIR, edited by JERRY THOMPSON
& EDDIE MULLER

ORANGE COUNTY NOIR, edited by GARY PHILLIPS

PALM SPRINGS NOIR, edited by
BARBARA DeMARCO-BARRETT

PARIS NOIR (FRANCE), edited by AURÉLIEN MASSON

PARIS NOIR: THE SUBURBS, edited by HERVÉ
DELOUCHE

PHILADELPHIA NOIR, edited by CARLIN ROMANO

PHOENIX NOIR, edited by PATRICK MILLIKIN

PITTSBURGH NOIR, edited by KATHLEEN GEORGE

PORTLAND NOIR, edited by KEVIN SAMPSELL

PRAGUE NOIR (CZECH REPUBLIC),
edited by PAVEL MANDYS

PRISON NOIR, edited by JOYCE CAROL OATES

PROVIDENCE NOIR, edited by ANN HOOD

QUEENS NOIR, edited by ROBERT KNIGHTLY

RICHMOND NOIR, edited by ANDREW BLOSSOM,
BRIAN CASTLEBERRY & TOM DE HAVEN

RIO NOIR (BRAZIL), edited by TONY BELLOTTO

ROME NOIR (ITALY), edited by CHIARA STANGALINO
& MAXIM JAKUBOWSKI

SAN DIEGO NOIR, edited by MARYELIZABETH HART

SAN FRANCISCO NOIR, edited by PETER MARAVELIS

SAN FRANCISCO NOIR 2: THE CLASSICS,
edited by PETER MARAVELIS

SAN JUAN NOIR (PUERTO RICO),
edited by MAYRA SANTOS-FEBRES

SANTA CRUZ NOIR, edited by SUSIE BRIGHT

SANTA FE NOIR, edited by ARIEL GORE

SÃO PAULO NOIR (BRAZIL),
edited by TONY BELLOTTO

SEATTLE NOIR, edited by CURT COLBERT

SINGAPORE NOIR, edited by CHERYL LU-LIEN TAN

SOUTH CENTRAL NOIR, edited by GARY PHILLIPS

STATEN ISLAND NOIR, edited by PATRICIA SMITH

ST. LOUIS NOIR, edited by SCOTT PHILLIPS

STOCKHOLM NOIR (SWEDEN), edited by
NATHAN LARSON & CARL-MICHAEL EDENBORG

ST. PETERSBURG NOIR (RUSSIA), edited by
NATALIA SMIRNOVA & JULIA GOUMEN

SYDNEY NOIR (AUSTRALIA), edited by JOHN DALE

TAMPA BAY NOIR, edited by COLETTE BANCROFT

TEHRAN NOIR (IRAN), edited by SALAR ABDOH

TEL AVIV NOIR (ISRAEL), edited by ETGAR KERET
& ASSAF GAVRON

TORONTO NOIR (CANADA), edited by JANINE ARMIN
& NATHANIEL G. MOORE

TRINIDAD NOIR (TRINIDAD & TOBAGO), edited by LISA
ALLEN-AGOSTINI & JEANNE MASON

TRINIDAD NOIR: THE CLASSICS
(TRINIDAD & TOBAGO), edited by EARL LOVELACE
& ROBERT ANTONI

TWIN CITIES NOIR, edited by JULIE SCHAPER
& STEVEN HORWITZ

USA NOIR, edited by JOHNNY TEMPLE

VANCOUVER NOIR (CANADA), edited by SAM WIEBE

VENICE NOIR (ITALY), edited by MAXIM JAKUBOWSKI

WALL STREET NOIR, edited by PETER SPIEGELMAN

ZAGREB NOIR (CROATIA), edited by IVAN SRŠEN

FORTHCOMING

HAMBURG NOIR (GERMANY), edited by JAN KARSTEN

HONOLULU NOIR, edited by CHRIS McKINNEY

NATIVE NOIR, edited by DAVID HESKA WANBLI WEIDEN

SACRAMENTO NOIR, edited by JOHN FREEMAN

VIRGIN ISLANDS NOIR, edited by TIPHANIE YANIQUE
& RICHARD GEORGES

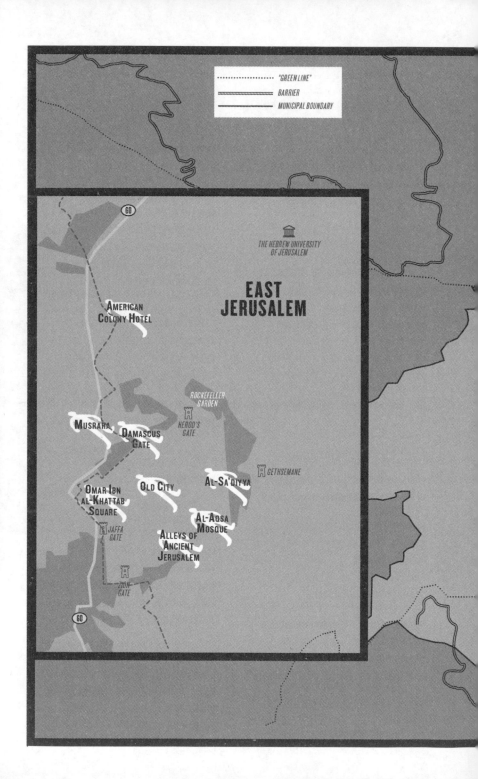

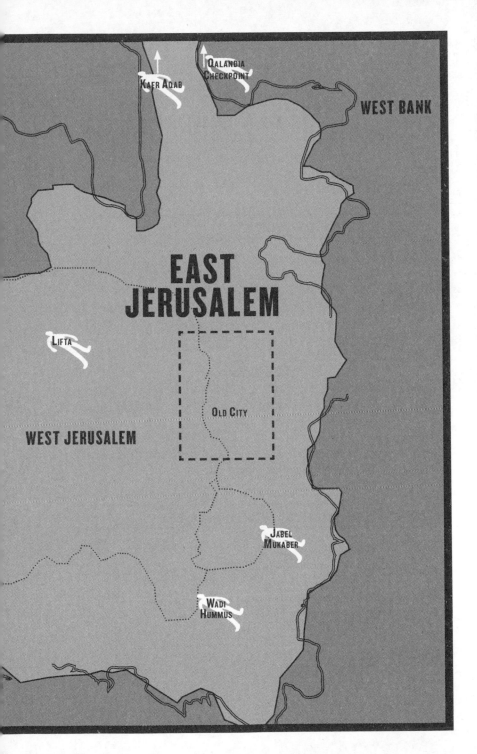

TABLE OF CONTENTS

PART III: MOVING INTO DESPAIR

INTRODUCTION
Opening the Black Box

Translated by Dr. Nazih Kassis

A friend of mine, the Palestinian writer Salman Natour, once said: "If you want to know a people, open their black box and read their literature," because literature is the mirror that reflects the peoples' memories, ordinary lives, extraordinary thoughts, and their dreams. But what if this literature is about "Jerusalem," the city that has embraced so many prophets? God probably gathered all the various peoples there in order to make them understand that they worship the same God!

The stones of this city, which was established seven thousand years ago, have spoken several languages, because the city has been attacked fifty-two times, occupied forty-four times, besieged twenty-three times, and destroyed twice. Over the centuries, Jerusalem has been populated by several peoples, including the Jebusites, the first Canaanite tribes, the Philistines/Palestinians, and the People of Israel; many have passed through and left behind witnesses to their civilizations in every corner of the city.

When you move through the streets of Jerusalem today, you will notice that history surrounds you from all sides. You hear Adhan, the Islamic call to prayer, recited by the muezzin from the Dome of the Rock; you hear the bells of the Church of the Holy Sepulchre, where the Christians pray, accompanied by the voices of the Jewish worshippers at the Wailing Wall. You are filled with awe and stand helpless to do anything except feel both joy and sadness at the same time. Your feelings mingle, your thoughts get confused, and you peer at the sky waiting for God's mercy and relief.

When Akashic Books invited me to edit this collection of short stories, I knew that the task would be difficult, that many people before me had not succeeded in doing this, and that caution is important with such a huge project. Despite the difficulties of the task, I did not hesitate because Jerusalem is a city I adore with all my heart and visit frequently because my day job is based there, near the Gate of the Column, near the sesame-sprinkled ovens of Jerusalemite cakes, near the radish and mint saleswomen who sit on the ground earning their living.

There, I leave my heart with Jews, Arabs, residents, visitors, and tourists who wander the streets drinking from Jerusalem's sanctity, smelling its incense, perfume, and spices, and drawing in their hearts their own map of the place.

My mission was not easy. It took a great deal of effort to persuade the writers to contribute their fiction stories to this collection. Then I had to edit the stories, send them out for translation, and review them again. Finally, after several years of work, we have succeeded in our goal.

The stories here are varied, and I did not interfere with the writers' content. I asked them to portray the city of Jerusalem as they live it, as they feel it, as they appreciate it, as they fear it, as they want it to be, and as they imagine it in the past, the present, and the future.

For example, the writer Ziad Khadash takes us on an escape from Assyrian soldiers in a beautiful work of historical fiction, which is answered by Iyad Shamasnah, who has written a story that is closer to science fiction, featuring a dream that cannot come true because of the particular time and place in which his characters find themselves. Thus, the dreams of the poor, which remain ink on paper, are demolished by the same bulldozer that demolishes houses, that demolishes the hopes of many in Ibrahim Jouhar's story.

Nearly every writer gives a different nickname to the city of Jerusalem-al-Quds. It is "the city of love and loss" in the story by Mahmoud Shukair, who has won several international awards; it is the city "where the prayers of worshippers and the hymns of the thankful rise in the air" in Nuzha al-Ramlawi's story; it is the city of "mosques, churches, falafel, mujaddara" according to Jameel al-Salhout; it is a city with "cameras in the ceiling" in Nuzha Abu Ghosh's tale; and in Rahaf al-Sa'ad's contribution the city is simply "extraordinary."

And now we put the black box in your hands! Kindly open it to reveal the secrets of Jerusalem and its people, who wake up to the sound of a forgotten rooster from a previous era to declare the beginning of a new dawn, so that life will not stop recording its diary entries.

Rawya Jarjoura Burbara
July 2023

PART I

Fatal Crossings

THE CEILING OF THE CITY

BY NUZHA ABU GHOSH

Damascus Gate

Translated by Catherine Cobham

The ceiling of the city was high and wide. Morning's chandelier cast a rosy light over the houses and alleyways.

He adjusted the mirror hanging in the middle of his room. Its frame was made of faded bamboo. He had bought it from a secondhand vendor in Jerusalem's Mahane Yehuda Market for twenty shekels. That was a day he would never forget.

He still remembered the glare and absurdity of the city in the eyes of the blond soldier when she grabbed the long rifle hanging over her shoulder and said sharply, "Step aside, please. Show me your ID."

God, why's she picking on me? he had thought.

"Why are you here?" she asked. "What's the reason for your visit to Jerusalem?"

"I was born in Jerusalem."

"Respect, Rahel!" her Ethiopian colleague interjected. "How did you know he was an Arab?"

"Don't you see how he drags his feet? And look at his shoes, and the cigarette packet."

The Ethiopian soldier's laughter filled the market.

He wanted to tell her the proverb his Aunt Wajiha

often quoted: *God have mercy. You only got to the palace yesterday afternoon.* But he felt the words would stick in his throat.

When he took out the mirror that day to show the male soldier, as he'd been ordered, black whirlpools swirled around in it, perfectly reflecting those inside him. But today, when he looked in the same mirror, he saw little of what was in his heart and mind. He saw a new person that didn't look like him, so he tried to alter his appearance. He smiled, adjusted his hat, raised his eyebrows, and stroked his mustache, but in spite of this, all he could see was a bald man with thick eyebrows, a profuse beard, and a distracted expression. He didn't know why the mirror was resisting him and his reality.

He felt the emptiness in him spreading and becoming increasingly indifferent.

Suddenly, he heard distant bells and a strange echo ringing in his ears. He muttered, "The only way I can fill this emptiness is to pray in al-Aqsa Mosque."

As he reached the steps of the Damascus Gate, a soldier stopped him: "ID, please."

He looked at his shoes and packet of cigarettes, then turned around, took a deep breath, and pointed to his own chest. He opened his eyes wide, raised his brows, and asked in annoyance, "Me? Do you mean *me?*"

"Don't ask questions." The soldier's voice was harsh. "ID, please."

He began to turn out his pockets, once, twice, three times, but didn't find the ID card. Embarrassed, he said,

"I left it in my suit when I went to my neighbor's son's wedding yesterday."

Another soldier, rifle raised, yelled, "Face the wall! Don't move!"

Where's your ID? Face the wall? Don't move? In my own country? On my own doorstep? On my land, and the land of my fathers? O world, people, nation, there is no god but God. I'm from Jerusalem. I swear to Almighty God that I was born in Jerusalem. The midwife Umm As'ad can testify. Everyone knows me. Ask anyone in this city and they will tell you who I am. I am Sa'id bin Umar bin 'Ata bin Marzuq, Jerusalem born and bred. Why are you aiming that gun at me? What have I done to you? I'm a peaceful person on my way to al-Aqsa. To pray. I've traveled all over the world and nobody has harassed me about my ID. And now you come to my city and tell me not to move!

Two soldiers grabbed his arms, handcuffed him, and shoved him into a military vehicle. "We're going to take you to the Russian compound," one said. "We'll confirm your identity there."

I don't want to go! Untie me! Don't push me. Let me breathe, let me smell the fresh air!

He scowled and felt strangely dizzy and began using his feet to defend himself. Foam came out of his mouth. He wanted to say, *You give me your ID cards. I want to know which country each of you came from.* But the words stuck to his tongue, his voice shook, and all that came out were disjointed grunts: "You came from . . . Pol-an-d, Eeeth-iopia . . . Rus-sia . . . you . . . ah ah . . . no no no."

Seven minutes later he arrived at the Russian compound, the Maskobiyeh Detention Center. They shoved him in with three other detainees. When he heard them speaking Arabic, he warmed to them.

"Thank God you're Arabs."

"That's right," said one of the men. "I'm from a village in the Nablus district. This is my cousin, he's from Hebron. And this man here is from the Ramallah area. They caught us in Jerusalem, inside a workshop, working without a permit."

"I'm from Jerusalem," he explained. "They held me because I didn't have my ID on me. I left it in my suit yesterday."

The detainees laughed theatrically. "You forgot your blue ID, did you, dear?! You Jerusalemites really think you're better than everyone else. No one can match you! You wander freely through the city, wherever you please."

Through their laughter, he spoke up: "What's a blue ID?"

"Blue has different rhythms, my friend. I mean, is it light blue, dark blue, or navy?" The man from Nablus cracked up. "It has a menorah printed on it, or a Star of David. No . . . more likely the blue and white flag." Roars of laughter. "Anyway, blue is better than West Bank green."

Sa'id bin Umar bin 'Ata bin Marzuq felt his face muscles contract, and he began searching for relief in the emptiness that was inside him that morning. But all he found were a bunch of intertwining threads that nobody in the world could untangle.

When he left the prison that evening, he tried to hide

the hot tears sliding down his cheeks, afraid they'd be captured by the cameras in the ceiling of the city.

THE SCORPION

BY IBRAHIM JOUHAR
Old City

Translated by Sawad Hussain

I f it weren't for that monstrous scorpion on the back of that massive truck, it would have been like any other day in Jerusalem. *Ordinary* in Jerusalem means a lot of questions and clashes—and some blood, from humans or even stones. Stones bleed too, they have feelings, tears. Today, the scorpion will be responsible for blood flowing, screams rising, and a sadness heavy enough to burrow into the depths of one's chest—for how long, only God knows. And yet, some of this sadness may leak out in the form of anguished voices and tears, tears that escape despite one's best efforts. *I tell myself I am used to seeing the clouds of dust rise after the razing of a neighbor's house. I watch thick clouds of dust rising, roiling upward, only to return and inhabit people's hearts.*

"Don't cry! You don't have the right to. Crying is for those who feel helpless, those who can't find a way out."

"What should I do, then? How can I not be sad seeing dreams fall to pieces and stones bleed in this place? Tell me, what should I do?"

"Just don't cry, that's the most important thing . . ."

The conversation was cut short by a more pressing matter, a nonnegotiable one: "Vacate the house. You've got to clear out in ten minutes. Got it? After that we'll start razing everything, even if you're still here. Hurry, move! No time for hanging around. Faster!"

He received the order while trying to shake off the remnants of sleep and dreams. What kind of morning was this? His tongue was paralyzed. It felt like dry wood. What could he say? And would anybody even listen? The echo of the sudden command resonated within: *Vacate the house.* The words got lost among their folds. But were they just words? He felt these words knocking violently on his face and his heart. They weren't just words; these ones could kill. He raised his hand to make up for his limp tongue and it let him down. *What can I say? Me, alone, cornered by police, orders, and bulldozers? Can words stop the greedy fangs of a bulldozer? How many houses with dreams, hopes, and tears have these fangs devoured?*

"But I have a lawyer who's working on—"

"Move it. There's no time. We're going to pull it all down. Five minutes left!"

Tears replaced dialogue. Children cast wondering glances. The wife wailed: "O wasted life, O lost dreams."

"Come on, faster!" The hateful words echoed off the nearby valley.

He collapsed in grief. Later he would thank God for the "blessed" concussion that spared him from having to watch his dreams crumble, preyed on by the bulldozer. A few minutes and the home was a pile of rubble. He couldn't save a single piece of furniture. He got both of his children and his wife out, and now he lay there unconscious as they wailed. As if in a nightmare, he tried to say something but couldn't find his tongue. He tried to scream but not a sound emerged. The dream had come to an end for two children who had hoped to live in a house that could contain their joy. If it hadn't been for that scorpion, the children would be fast asleep, content, advancing toward a better future. Scorpions don't like children; they don't like life itself. Scorpions live to prove the power of death to children who have yet to taste life.

If it hadn't been for that scorpion, then it would have been an ordinary day in a not-so-ordinary city. Students going to school, employees to their offices. They all would have been walking, heads bowed, preoccupied, pushing away the usual barrage of questions: *What does the day hold for me? Will I make it home this evening? Will my son come home safely? What will tomorrow bring?* Fear and anxiety were the currency in this grieving city. In the past few days, no one had been safe from the police in all their guises. Murder at the hands of an armed, tense officer was the slightest movement away. Panic began to creep among the people, and they asked themselves where their sense of safety had gone . . . But was it really this monstrous scorpion that had disturbed their serenity? Had there been any serenity to begin with? Was the scorpion alone responsible for muddying the waters flowing through their day? Or was something else responsible, something that no one had yet put their finger on?

You've got to clear out in ten minutes. Got it? That was the order.

And is ten minutes enough to carry my children and leave? Or to say farewell to my bedroom? Or . . . He cried. He cried—oppressed, empty handed, helpless. *Aren't I a human in this murderous world? O God, O God of people, O God of majesty, help us. Help us, O God. We're so weak with no hands, no tongues, and this scorpion is ruthless. This scorpion has no mercy, does not care about our tears. It's a scorpion, after all, and we're made of flesh and blood, hearts that love, cry, and break. Do hearts even cry? Indeed, they cry bitterly. Hearts cry, stones cry, the city cries. All this hateful scorpion has are fangs that know how to kill. No eyes to weep or a heart to grieve. O God.*

You've got to clear . . . The scorpion approached. The house still stood. The man dried his tears not wanting anyone to see. If only he could, he would close his eyes and turn away from the ugly scene. Nothing crueler than seeing your dream house in pieces . . .

I built it one stone at a time. I built it hoping to give my children a home, to protect them, to say, "This is my house. This is my house, everyone. I have a home now." This scorpion never crossed my mind. I was absorbed with laying one stone down next to its brother and so forth, one line atop the next. Then it was a house with walls, a roof, and rooms. I let go of the idea of a garden for the time being. I told myself, "I'll just have the walls and build a nice garden later. There's no house without a garden. The house should have a garden pulsing with life, roses, and a few fruit trees. Yes, it should." But then, the scorpion.

You've got to clear . . . Got to clear . . . Got to . . . And the letters of the words disappeared. Were they even words? They sounded like a hissing snake. A snake that bites, its venom polluting blood, its victim dying slowly.

There is nothing grimmer than such a death. And here he was today, his dreams dying to a monstrous scorpion. If this scorpion wasn't on the truck this morning, the machine of death and destruction, then the people of Jerusalem would have welcomed an ordinary day in their extraordinary existence—in their unusual city of checkpoints, accusations, and dying children. You in this city live day and night between knives, gunshots, and expressions of hatred and suspicion. *When will there be a house for us in this city?* he asked himself. *One of freedom and security?* Rambling, dreaming, hoping. Now the scorpion was leaving. It had leveled the dream house to the ground and was leaving with the truck.

Where is it going . . . O God, please protect the people and their homes from this scorpion. He broke into a fit of crying that could be heard from afar. Those who heard him bowed their heads.

The scorpion continued on its way to the next victim, and the next, and the next.

BETWEEN THE TWO JERUSALEMS

BY OSAMA ALAYSA

Lifta

Translated by Raphael Cormack

1

As far as I'm concerned—"I" being the journalist Osama Alaysa—there is no doubt that it was wrong for people to call him *al-Dabi'* ("hyena"). It wasn't just rude and disrespectful; it was also unintelligent. Their many shortcomings in the art of creating nicknames were clear. This was an art with a long and noble heritage in the cities and countryside of Palestine. In later years, some Orientalist scholars even became aware of it. Their curiosity was aroused when they noticed that people in this holy land had a habit of giving each other unholy nicknames, which, over time, turned into surnames, eventually becoming sources of pride to their descendants. These included, among others, *al-Aqra'* ("the bald"), *al-A'raj* ("the lame"), *al-Atrash* ("the deaf"), *Abu Naml* ("father of ants"), and *Abu Qaml* ("father of lice"). There were also others based on animals: *Sarsur* ("cockroach" or "cricket"), *Baghl* ("ox"), and *Jahsh* ("mule"). Then there was a third kind derived from plants: *Bamia* ("okra"), *Kusa* ("zucchini"), *Jazara* ("carrot"), and *Batikh* ("watermelon"). And a fourth kind, from professions: *al-*

Najjar ("carpenter"), *al-Hajjar* ("stonemason"), *al-Khayyat* ("tailor"), *al-Haddadin* ("blacksmiths"), *Qanawati* ("canal digger"), and so on. The Orientalists did their usual rounds of research and classification and eventually drew conclusions. They claimed that this culture of naming stretched back to the beginning of this land's history—from the time of biblical heroes, to the corrupt modern age with its political "heroes."

I dislike the nickname Hyena, but I definitely prefer it to the term more commonly used to describe people like him; they would lump them all together under "mongoloid," as if there were no differences between them. I hesitate to use that word here, since it is no longer scientifically accepted. The correct term to use is Down syndrome, named after John Langdon Down, who became the first person to describe the condition in 1862. He observed that children born with it had facial features, particularly around the eyes, that seemed to evoke the Mongolian race, hence the term. Without question, this explanation of the word "mongoloid" should incite discussion on the deep-seated racism of Down and the times he lived in.

But now is not the time for such discussion. I am trying to find out who first gave this refugee from Lifta the nickname Hyena. No one in Ramallah or al-Bireh knows. It appears that another journalist like me, who wanted to do an investigative piece, had already asked this question. But for most people who knew this man, it was not important. They did know that he was born into a family that fled Lifta, which had been annexed by the occupiers and used to set up public and governmental services for the nascent state of Israel, in what is now known as West Jerusalem. Through all this, the stone houses of the village stood steadfast, as did its spring that glistened in Wadi al-Shami. These served to remind the occupiers that they were taking what was not theirs. Looking at the remnants of Lifta during their commutes, they saw structures that looked just like the houses they had moved into, or the ones they'd destroyed to build European-style dwellings. The houses became part of the never-ending debate on what to do about the Arabic architectural heritage of the occupied land. There were arguments between environmental organizations on one side and the government on the other, which wanted to finish off whatever remained of the village and erect villas—at least this was what Prime Minister Sharon had suggested. He wanted to widen the streets and remove any trace of the old, make everything appear as if it had just descended from some European sky. So that people could no longer tell that this was Lifta, where men used to throw gold at their wives' sandals because their hands were overflowing with wealth, or so the story goes. (Perhaps this little story explains the famous strength of the village women, which unsettles those who dillydally in the sidewalk cafés of Ramallah and al-Bireh.)

The people of Lifta strenuously deny these stories. They say that the people telling them are confused. It has nothing to do with sewing gold coins into sandals, or any other shoes for that matter. The origin of this myth is simply that they used to sew fine gold thread into their shoes. It is related to a local style of *thobe* known as "heaven and hell," so called because they are embroidered with green and red silk. Some women would stitch gold threads into them as a sign of their husbands' wealth.

Just before the Nakba, Lifta had become a rich place. Its quarries sourced much of the stone needed for Jerusalem's houses, and it actively traded with local Jewish neighborhoods, selling tons of fruits and vegetables. Two young men from the village, graduates of the American University of Beirut, opened two clinics. And two cafés sprung up, products of the burgeoning leisure and entertainment industry that grew in the Holy Land in the first half of the twentieth century. These cafés attracted the denizens of Jerusalem and other surrounding areas, but it is unclear what happened in them. We know a little about them from one of the great intellectuals of the age, Khalil al-Sakakini, who wrote that he went with two friends to a café in Lifta in 1941. "We smoked"—that was the extent of his description.

The Zionist Haganah attacked one of these cafés with Sten guns, killing seven people and wounding many others. This marked the beginning of the expulsion of the population. When the Zionist gangs had accomplished what they wanted, Ben-Gurion came from Tel Aviv on a Saturday, shattering its holiness, happy that Lifta had been emptied of its Arab inhabitants. It was the realization of his dream to remove that thorn in his side, the ancient and continuous presence of Arabs, in favor of Jewish neighborhoods and settlements. This would soon lead to the Nakba, which, for the first time in history, divided Jerusalem into two parts—East and West.

Inspired by these historic moments, Ben-Gurion addressed the Mapai party leadership on February 7, 1948, in Jerusalem: "From your entry into Jerusalem through Lifta-Romema, through Mahane Yehuda, King George Street, and Mea Shearim—there are no strangers left. One hundred percent Jews. Since Jerusalem's destruction in the days of the Romans—it hasn't been so Jewish as it is now. In many Arab districts in the West—one sees not one Arab."

The Arabs had disappeared from Lifta, and from Malha, al-Qatamun, Ein Kerem, Suba, al-Qastal, Beit Mahsir, Baq'a, Talbiya, Deir Yassin, Sataf, and other Arab villages and neighborhoods. No sooner had the Nakba come than the rural villages became suburbs, another step in merging them with the Jewish settlements. All of this happened despite the good relationship between Lifta and other villages, despite nonaggression pacts, despite notable interreligious marriages.

As time passed, the occupying government began to regard Lifta's ruins as part of the terrain, as a piece of Jewish heritage in the Promised Land. They looked into making the site an open-air center for the study of natural history, to strengthen Jewish connection to this picturesque location.

Eventually, the occupiers settled the matter once and for all by placing a large sign in front of the village, declaring it a nature reserve. It became common to glimpse Jewish men and women enjoying themselves by the spring in their swimsuits or lying in the shade of the fig trees. The village mosque was converted into a ritual purification pool for menstruating women.

The once-impressive houses still remain. Not just their stone exteriors, but also their inside features: paintings, traditional colored tiles, cement floors, room divisions. The occupying government numbered them all, fenced them off with barbed wire, and put signs on them asserting that they are property of Israel and that any entry is forbidden, punishable by law.

The houses on the western slope of the mountain are inhabited by birds. Hikers or settlers, motivated by desire or curiosity, will sometimes sneak into them, but they do not stay. On the eastern slope, the occupying police have struggled to keep the houses secure: their doors and windows are gone, and a mix of vagrants, artists, bohemians, and yogis are installed in them on a temporary or permanent basis, living simply.

Lifta has increasingly been embraced as historically important, and as you read this, it is likely to soon be a UNESCO World Heritage site, as the location of the biblical Mey Naftoah. Even if the Hyena's relatives get angry and protest that it is *their* country and *their* heritage.

2

Sorry, let us get back to the Hyena, so we don't lose him and his story the way Lifta was lost!

Many people do not understand how such a ferocious moniker was given to a man known for his gentleness. Eventually, though, his nickname evolved from Dabi' to Dab'oo (or *Deboo*, as the westernized women of Ramallah pronounced it, which better suited this short man with long flowing hair and asymmetrical facial features that barely changed whether he was happy or sad).

If you had to guess, you would surely say that he was called Hyena because of the fear he aroused. But as he walked the streets of Ramallah or al-Bireh, casually stopping in front of shops, talking and joking, no one understood at first why such a calm and tender being had been given the (apparently!) cute nickname Hyena.

He reinforced the stereotype that people with Down syndrome were always creative or gifted in a certain field. Like Mazen, the wedding singer, who was known for his attention to personal hygiene and creaseless clothes, ironed down to his socks and underwear. He never left a wedding without standing next to the band, singer, or deejay and playing the air oud, plucking invisible strings and swaying in time to the music. When he had tired the singer out, he would grab the mic and sing himself. When he was at peak performance, people who did not understand anything coming out of his mouth started to laugh. This became his party trick. Wedding guests would wait for it and sometimes actively encourage it. For people who only came to weddings out of social or family obligation, his singing made the evening fun.

Dab'oo, for his part, was passionate about impersonating traffic policemen. At first he did it timidly, but before long, whenever there was a traffic jam at a crossroads, he would stand in the middle of the street and direct cars. He experienced a sense of power when he saw the drivers in Ramallah and al-Bireh obeying the movements of his hands. To stop a vehicle or let it pass with just a wave gave him a pleasure like no other. No one understood the feeling it gave him. Likewise, they did not understand his feelings toward the opposite sex, even though café patrons, shopkeepers, and various others debated the topic endlessly.

Dab'oo managed to establish himself as an unofficial traffic officer. Initially, he met with opposition from the Israeli police and border guards, who had come to the West Bank and Gaza because of the growing popular resistance to the occupation. This was during those strange few years before the First Intifada broke out. Dab'oo's position was formalized after the creation of the Palestinian Authority, as Ramallah and al-Bireh grew rapidly, in both size and population. It helped that he had visited the first governor of the district, a refugee from Lifta like himself. They say that this representative of the new authority gave Dab'oo a military uniform out of gratitude for his services to the resistance. He was delighted to receive the khaki uniform. At a kiosk on al-Irsal Street, he found a metal badge with an eagle on it and the colors of the Palestinian flag; it looked perfect pinned to his shirt.

He was lucky to get that badge. In those days, people were not too interested in the Palestinian flag. It had been banned before the Palestinian Authority came into being, and youths who had raised it on transmission towers or in demonstrations paid with their lives; Israeli bullets did not look kindly on this national symbol. So, unsurprisingly, people would get emotional when they saw it fluttering in the wind. Interest in it had declined in favor of other flags—each faction had its own. It was sometimes

hard for people to distinguish between all the flags, especially since most of them recycled the same ideas.

Dab'oo's attempts to establish himself as a traffic officer in this new era were not without problems. On several
occasions, the newly formed police force took him to the
station near the Manara roundabout, despite his protesta-
tions that the governor had given him the khaki uniform;
it was a permit for him to do his job and they could not
take it away from him. Some saw his presence, standing
in front of the police station next to the coffee stand, as
symbolic of the new authority, which could not tell the
good from the bad. He was a poor, innocent man who was
just having harmless fun. The policemen, whether they
already knew him or had just started serving in Ramallah
and al-Bireh, would hardly need to talk to him to realize
that he did not need to be investigated and should be
released immediately.

3

Dab'oo triumphed over all efforts to stop him from working. His popularity grew. In time, many others took on
the role of traffic officer, driven by necessity and a sense
of responsibility. Like Abu Saadi, a beloved, wizened old
man, who came as a refugee from the destroyed village of
Deir Aban in the central hills to Turmus Ayya, known for
its beautiful villas and red-tile roofs. The village had been
built on remittances from America. It was one of the ear-
liest to be hit by the plague of overseas migration. They
say it was the ticket seller Hanna al-Sa' who started the
exodus when he went to Istanbul with a group of Greek

pilgrims. Then, before the end of the nineteenth century, Youssef al-Dibini began the movement to the Americas, which became an epidemic in Ramallah, al-Bireh, and the villages of the surrounding countryside.

The most important event, a turning point in the history of migration in Ramallah, came when Isa Eida, an emigrant to Brazil, sent a hundred gold pounds to his father. This is said to be the first remittance of its kind to come to Ramallah. For a long time after, locals celebrated its arrival; they went to Eida's house with well-wishes and congratulations.

The women of Ramallah used to pray that Isa Eida and Youssef al-Dibini might open the wide gates of emigration to their husbands. Their sad songs rang out in the corners of their houses:

Let's travel away, go take me with you
I have only dukkah for breakfast
I can put up with being hungry
But I can't put up with being apart

And when people came back, the women of Ramallah would sing this song:

Welcome, traveler from the Jerusalem road
With a gold watch that makes sounds like a pipe
Welcome, traveler from the Jerusalem road
Wearing a gold watch, looking fine in fancy clothes

Abu Saadi, the traffic officer, wore a black-and-white

kaffiyeh, a black-striped suit. He sometimes put a small crown with a picture of Yasser Arafat on his agal and a rose in his buttonhole. He was a familiar face at marches and demonstrations; when the minister Eyyad Abu Ain was killed in a confiscated part of Turmus Ayya, Abu Saadi was next to him. He was beaten by Israeli soldiers too.

Abu Saadi was nicknamed Rebel Citizen, Octogenarian Fighter, and Sheikh of the Struggle. If you saw him directing traffic with noble and worthy intentions, you wouldn't think that he was overflowing with revolutionary nationalism. He could be seen at the Manara roundabout, calmly directing traffic and helping people across the road. But even this had a patriotic motive: if the Israeli enemies saw that Palestine was well organized, they would think twice before messing with them.

Abu Saadi did not threaten Dab'oo's position as king of Ramallah's traffic, even if Dab'oo was sometimes annoyed by his encroachment. At least that's what some people have told me, without explaining how they knew. Dab'oo himself does not speak much; he mostly just laughs and smiles. When he does speak, it is often hard to understand. Those who spend time with him understand him through gestures, movements, and expressions.

The person who really threatened Dab'oo's throne was a new, young, official traffic control officer—Ra'id Abu Awwad. He appeared at the Manara roundabout in his well-fitting blue uniform; his strange and extravagant way of directing traffic became the subject of much discussion among locals. Articles written about Abu Awwad called him the "dancing cop" or "twirling cop" because he was always turning his body as he moved his hands, so that he could signal to vehicles as directly and accurately as possible. Local television channels loved him. They thought him innovative, dynamic, artistic. And the police department loved him too, giving him an official award for his efforts.

With this new man in town, people began to forget Dab'oo. Did no one remember how he'd misdirect Israeli border guards at the roundabout to protect protesters? Did they forget khaki-clad Dab'oo, who had saved the lives of so many students? I tell you, Ramallah and al-Bireh weren't what they used to be.

The few people who still remembered Dab'oo's heroic and patriotic deeds supported him, subtly, by undermining Abu Awwad. They brought up the existence of another dancing cop who was famous among drivers in Abdali, an area in Jordan's capital, Amman, and before then in Ras al-Ein. They said that Abu Awwad was just copying this more talented Jordanian policeman.

I had actually seen that energetic Jordanian traffic cop. He was older than Abu Awwad but could perform skillful movements with much less tension and stress; his younger counterpart moved with too much haste and urgency. What is more, Hazza Thneibat (that's his name) always had a smile on his face when he worked, but the award-winning Palestinian cop wore an expression of exaggerated seriousness that seemed fake.

I hope Abu Awwad doesn't get annoyed if he ever reads this comparison. He surely wouldn't expect these words from a friend. He might complain or demand an apology, but I'm just trying to explain how things were and give you a vivid picture. I'm writing a short story about Dab'oo, so I need to create atmosphere. I've been forced to write something literary because it's impossible to write a piece of investigative journalism about the "Dab'oo incident." Everyone I interviewed told different, often contradictory stories. Some even denied that anyone with his name or description ever walked the streets of Ramallah and al-Bireh, those twin towns whose precise borders no one but the municipal cleaners know.

4

But come on, let's get back to Dab'oo and see what happened after Ra'id Abu Awwad turned up. We find him almost hopeless about returning to his old role. On the bright side, forgotten as he was, almost nobody saw him unsuccessfully trying to imitate Abu Awwad's performance in front of the school, or in front of the Gamal Abdel Nasser Mosque. Those who did pitied him.

Dab'oo came to terms with his new status as someone who wandered aimlessly—around Manara Square, Yasser Arafat Square, the souk, al-Irsal Street, Rukab Street . . . Before we go any further, I should say, or rather emphasize, that there may not be a grain of truth in this story of mine. But here it goes. This is where the story really begins.

One day, someone—I will refrain from mentioning his name—was driving past with Israeli license plates. He saw Dab'oo in his khaki uniform, sipping a soda, filled with hatred for the world and curses for the people of Ramallah and al-Bireh.

"Dab'oo!" he shouted. "What are you doing? Get in the car and come to Jerusalem!"

So Dab'oo got in and they rode from the besieged city of Ramallah to the besieged city of Jerusalem, which Dab'oo hadn't visited in many years. The soldiers at the Qalandia checkpoint did not ask for his ID, which was lucky because he didn't have it on him. At any rate, he belonged to that large "mongoloid" tribe, whose IDs are their faces.

When they arrived at the Damascus Gate, Dab'oo got out and the driver walked off by himself. Dab'oo was alone. A group of children crowded around, asking him questions that he did not seem to understand:

"Are you from the West Bank?"

"Are you from Gaza?"

"Are you an Arab-Israeli?"

"Are you a Jerusalemite like us?"

"Are you a bedouin?"

"Are you a fella from the north, from the south, from somewhere far, far away?"

Then he wandered around the old walls of Jerusalem. Suddenly, a Jewish prostitute jumped out from behind some bushes, high on drugs. In broken Arabic she explained her services: a kiss (price dependent on location and duration), touching and fondling, all the way up to the main event. But she couldn't understand him. "What? You stupid Arab . . . you expect a good time for free?"

As he got close to the Jaffa Gate and the busy roads

there, something changed in him. He regained all the passion and verve he thought he had lost. He was a real hyena, he told himself, imprisoned in a cage for years and now released into the wild. He saw so many vehicles and traffic jams that he began to feel free again. This was his playground, home of his love and his passion. Amid all this noise, he found himself. He became lord of the streets.

He came across a jam that was so much bigger than anything he'd seen in Ramallah or al-Bireh. Passing vehicles of all kinds, he walked to the junction that separated the two Jerusalems, divided by war then united by war. Jerusalem, in the eyes of the world, was split into Israeli Jerusalem and Arab Jerusalem, but in reality Israel controlled both parts.

And everyone had forgotten the indescribable favor that Lifta and the village of Mallaha had done for stone-walled Jerusalem. They extended this city of mosques and churches into land beyond its suffocating old walls, into the modern age.

Dab'oo stood in the jam. Around him were Jaffa Street, Mamilla, Hebron Road, New Gate, Jaffa Gate, and the long walls. He moved his hands and body, sometimes copying the dancing cop from the Manara roundabout, sometimes doing his own moves. He succeeded, up to a point. But his whole life seemed to be a long series of surprises and misunderstandings. Here, too, things started to unravel. An Israeli woman saw the strange figure that Dab'oo cut among the traffic, then noticed that he was wearing the uniform of the Palestinian Authority. She must have had exceptional sight, because she picked out the red, white, green, and black on his badge. If she hadn't already won first prize in some international eyesight competition, she certainly deserved to. Her eyes could prove to the country, region, and world some of the undiscovered abilities of the Semitic race (at least the Jewish part of it).

What happened to Dab'oo at the border between the two Jerusalems is conjecture, like the rest of this story. I say this to protect myself against those who will read this story and ask if its characters and events are true—the one question people always ask.

Anyway, that eagle-eyed woman called the police and told them to arrest that damned Palestinian, the fake cop who was surely a terrorist on a mission. Soon, the real cops showed up and led Dab'oo to the Miskuwiya police station, which stands partly on old lands of Lifta, as do the central bus station, the Knesset, and a number of expensive hotels.

Upon starting the investigation, the police realized they had no idea what was going on. They checked the security cameras installed all over Jerusalem. They called in the prostitute, who said she remembered a mongoloid Arab who had told her clearly that he was a terrorist and saboteur. She said that she hadn't notified the police stationed all around her place of work because they would never have believed her. She had a complex relationship with the police: they loathed her, even though she insisted that she loved them. Anyway, she had faith that they would quickly arrest him without her help, so she had no need to interfere. This trust, the prostitute claimed, was yet more evidence of her love.

The cops also questioned the boys who had accosted Dab'oo at the Damascus Gate. Those nasty brats said that they had noticed he was a stranger and gathered around him, then they recognized that he wasn't from Jerusalem like them. They wanted to know what kind of Arab he was. If they had known that he was from *al-Hashtahim* ("the territories," the occupied West Bank), they would definitely have reported him. The parents cursed their children for causing problems and dragging them to this interrogation center.

After both his scheduled and random beatings (every policeman who entered the room slapped or punched him), Dab'oo was handed over to the security agency, Shin Bet. These people, who were more than a little arrogant, did not know where to start with this tired, thrashed soul. They pulled him from the interrogation room and made him stand next to the door with his hands raised against the wall. A Druze soldier appeared and grabbed Dab'oo in a warm embrace. He remembered him from the First Intifada.

"You were throwing stones at us, we were shooting bullets at you!" He laughed, then said, "You weren't the only mongoloid . . . We were all mongoloids and still are. How did you end up here? If those interrogators understood anything, they'd make a peace treaty with you and put an end to the fighting between your side and theirs."

Dab'oo was encouraged by the sudden appearance of a friendly face and began to mutter a few incomprehensible words. The soldier took this to mean that Dab'oo both recognized him and understood what he was talking about. As for the interrogators, they breathed a sigh of relief after hours investigating Dab'oo's infiltration of Jerusalem. His escapade had managed to score an important point in the game of national security (as they put it). He had found a way into Jerusalem and exposed the weaknesses of their well-trained police force. Then, within a few minutes, he had managed to direct traffic on a busy street.

Dab'oo had a green ID card like the other residents of Gaza and the West Bank. They used to have orange cards before the Palestinian Authority was created. Back then, they were not forbidden from moving between the lands of Palestine. But in the 1980s, the Shin Bet came up with a way to identify those who were actively opposing the occupation, so they could be subject to arrest, beatings, imprisonment: the green ID. This allowed soldiers at checkpoints to identify them and limit their movement. Since the creation of the Palestinian Authority, all Palestinians under it have been given a green card, which forbids them from entering Jerusalem or the lands occupied in 1948, except under special circumstances. Officials are given a VIP card that allows them to move through the lands, but even they live under the constant threat that their cards will be temporarily suspended or completely withdrawn.

5

In the security offices of Ramallah, which the media describes as the temporary capital of the future Palestinian state (always leaving out al-Bireh), the phone lit up. The officers put it on speaker and listened to their Israeli counterparts on the other end.

"We didn't know that when you tried to liberate Jerusalem you would send us Dab'oo . . ."

The officers in Ramallah laughed. "And how about you? We didn't know that Dab'oo alone would make you lie down and surrender . . ."

"Ha ha, we are waiting for the results of your investigations so we can include them in our case file and learn our lesson!"

Dab'oo was detained for a few more hours, not for further investigation but to coordinate his return to Ramallah. The convoy set off from the Miskuwiya police station with border guards to the front and rear and Dab'oo in a car with Shin Bet officers. Upon reaching the Qalandia checkpoint, they waited for the Palestinian vehicles to arrive at this sensitive location, usually off-limits to Palestinian security vehicles and officers.

At first, the Palestinian investigation had not been able to ascertain who took him to Jerusalem, how he or she did it, or why. Dab'oo's intentions had been noble, the investigators were sure of that. But other malign intentions could lie behind the incident, aimed at embarrassing the Palestinian Authority and its ability to maintain order and security.

The Palestinian security forces were relatively new, but after a while they proved their worth, discovering the identity of the driver. This was thanks to the large number of "delegates"—the Palestinian Authority's word for "intelligence officers"—working on the case. The driver spoke freely. He said that it just came to his head randomly, as a bit of fun. He couldn't remember what made him think to do it. He just randomly shouted to Dab'oo to get in his car and come to Jerusalem. "I wish that God had paralyzed my tongue before I said it," he told the investigators. But that devilish impulse was all there was to it. He was ready to submit to any investigation and face the consequences. This was, after all, his duty as a Palestinian.

But after a few days they closed the investigation. The driver left, with bruises on his face and neck, after signing a document confirming that he hadn't been subjected to torture. This piece of paper was to protect the Palestinian Authority, so that they couldn't be taken advantage of by the many human rights organizations with foreign agendas, who lie in ambush for claims of ill treatment of prisoners.

From that point forward, on the road to and from Jerusalem, the driver would avoid Dab'oo if he saw him. On the rare occasion that their eyes met, the two would smile at each other, acknowledging the secret that only they knew. This was a secret that could not be revealed to states or governments, which come and go across the centuries, believing they know everything about Palestine. The history books always ignore the little secrets that run through veins and live in bodies. But these secrets are what stay in the land forever. Perhaps that's why mothers tell their sad, angry children who want to emigrate that states and governments are bound by the laws of change and decay. However long they last, it is not forever.

IN AN EXTRAORDINARY CITY

BY RAHAF AL-SA'AD

Wadi Hummus

Translated by Nancy Roberts

July 22, 2019, 2:30 a.m.

The sound of bullets filled the sky above Jerusalem's Wadi Hummus neighborhood. It was only 2:30 in the morning, but the gunfire and tear gas canisters announced the arrival of the Israeli occupation army.

A little boy, not yet two years old, lurched in a fright and wakened his father with his crying and wordless stammers. All the father could do was jump up and shut the windows before the fumes could reach his wife and children.

Umm Muhammad, who'd gotten up to worship during the night, and was pleading with God for relief from yesterday's demolition decree, interrupted her prayer, terrified by the noise. Forced to block her nose from the stench of tear gas and gunpowder, she'd hardly had a chance to raise her hands in supplication and make her requests of God.

"What's going on? What are all these soldiers doing here?"

"I don't understand. How could they have come this fast?"

"This is crazy—the court rejected our petition against

the demolition order just yesterday morning! It hasn't even been twenty-four hours!"

"So why are they here? We've got nowhere else to go."

"Nobody's going to kick us out. They can demolish my house over my dead body. This house isn't just bricks and mortar. It's my sweat and blood, my life, my dignity! I'd sooner die than see it in ruins."

"So what do we do, Baba? They're armed to the teeth."

"We'll stand up to them . . . Wake up your brothers and sisters and warn the neighbors! Take off your jackets and wrap them around your mouths so you don't choke on the gas and smoke. We'll resist until they're gone for good."

Shouting "Allahu Akbar!" the boys gathered with their father around the door, pushing with all their might as the soldiers pressed from the other side. After making an opening in the door, the soldiers threw a tear gas canister inside.

"You've got ten minutes to vacate the house," a soldier barked. "Once the ten minutes are up, we'll destroy it and everything inside, even you!"

A month and a half earlier
The High Court of Justice had issued a decision to demolish facilities that, by the standards of the law, were "near the wall," on the pretext that they threatened public security. In concrete terms, this meant the demolition of ten residential buildings and one hundred apartments.

The morning after the court issued its decision, Abu Muhammad sat waiting for the lawyer in his office. For some time now, this issue was all he'd been able to think about. It was a matter of life and death. He'd stopped going to work, instead spending night and day at the lawyer's office. Every minute that passed weighed on his soul like a countdown to his own death.

When the lawyer arrived, he met Abu Muhammad with a cheery smile that seemed out of place under the circumstances, especially after the court's ruling. However, he seemed genuinely optimistic.

Abu Muhammad dispensed with the usual polite talk: "So, has there been some good development? That smile of yours can't be coming out of nowhere! Tell me what's going on."

"Well," the lawyer replied, "they've asked us to provide alternatives to demolishing your homes that would maintain the needed security around the separation wall. So that's what we'll do."

"But we don't know of any alternatives."

"Well, I do."

"Oh really? Like what?"

"I spent all night thinking, and I've come up with some simple solutions. But their presentation will decide how the judge responds. You also need to understand that in order for this to happen, you'll have to put out a bit."

"Pay, you mean? I'll pay whatever you want and more!"

"You won't be paying me, but rather somebody trusted in their eyes."

"What are you getting at?"

"I'll prepare a file for you laying out alternative solutions. Then you'll take it to a retired army officer who still works with the military and legal establishment. If you can get his signed approval, our petition will have a better chance of succeeding."

"And I have to pay this officer to sign it?"

"Exactly. This is the only option we've got left."

"In other words, in order to save my house, I have to get the approval of the people who stole it, and on top of that, pay them whatever they want. That's ridiculous!"

"Believe me, there's no other way."

The proposed solutions were to increase the height of the separation wall and activate more surveillance cameras in the area, and Abu Muhammad would have to appease the officer to certify these steps. Despite his resistance to the idea, he did what had been asked of him. For a puny signature, he had to pay no small price. Even so, it wasn't too much to be delivered from injustice.

Abu Muhammad's wife and companion for so many years had shared his dream of owning a house, an apartment, or even a small nest, anywhere in Jerusalem. They'd dreamed of providing for their children what they'd never had themselves. They wanted them to have a decent life, something to call their own that could spare them the woes of instability, a place to gather after they'd built their own nests. So would they have to scrimp on their dreams too? Or would it have been better not to have dreamed in the first place?

All this came to mind as Abu Muhammad awaited an outcome that, for all he knew, wouldn't really change anything. He thought about the hope he'd planted in the

hearts of his wife, his children, and possibly others concerned with the issue. Had the hope been a mirage? Had
it been unfair of him to induce hope for something he
couldn't guarantee? Or had he been right to bring some
peace of mind to their hearts after all the tension they'd
endured?

Waiting for the ruling was hard. Is it harder to wait
for something you know is coming, or for something you
can't even identify?

On June 11, the proposals offered by the residents and
endorsed by the high-ranking army officer were rejected
by the High Court of Justice. Thus, the original decision
to demolish all facilities near the wall was referred to the
relevant authorities and enforcement agencies.

"You have one month to demolish these buildings.
Otherwise, we'll demolish them ourselves. The Supreme
Court's decision calls for the demolition of all installa-
tions near the wall due to the threat they pose to the
internal security and public order of the State of Israel.
If you fail to demolish the facilities, we'll do it ourselves
when the deadline runs out, and you'll have to pay the
demolition fine."

"So now it's called a *facility*? Tell the judge, the officer, and the soldier that this is my *home*. It's my stake
in this city, what I worked hard for since I was young!
I've dreamed of owning a house in Jerusalem since I was
a kid. Is my house bothering you now? Is it a threat to
your security? Me? Am *I* threatening your security?! How
could I possibly threaten you when I can't even threaten
my wife with divorce? I'd have to pay a huge severance

dowry, and I've got nothing to pay it with. All I have is this house and my dignity. And now you want to take it all away from me. O Lord, do you hear me? O God, grant me justice, and don't leave me at the mercy of my oppressor!"

When he got home, Abu Muhammad didn't utter a word. All he wanted was to go to sleep and wake up on a day without injustice or oppression, without the occupation or demolitions or bombings, a day with no police sirens blaring, no gunshots ringing out. He wished he could wake up in Jerusalem, in his own house, without all the other circumstances. Without the court's decision and the futile petitions.

"So, what was the decision?" asked Umm Muhammad.

"We've got a month."

"A month to do what?"

"To demolish our house . . . before they do."

"What? They want us to demolish our house with our own hands? To take it apart stone by stone?"

"There's still a chance . . . We'll petition for a deferment based on—"

"Another petition? We've already got a new court and a new ruling, with the same result as always. Do you really still have hope? Let's get out of here . . . I'm tired of all this. Let's escape with our lives, migrate, and never come back."

"What? Abandon our home? You want to give up our life here, Umm Muhammad?"

"These are stones—that's all they are."

"That's exactly what they want us to do. They want

this whole city to turn into stones. They want us to turn into a heap of rubble."

"But can't you see? That's what we already are."

"No! Not yet. I've still got life and breath in me, and as long as I do, I'm going to resist."

"And so am I!"

"So you're with me?"

"I'm with you, but—"

"Nothing's more precious than Jerusalem, Umm Muhammad. There's no price too dear for it, even people's lives. So I'm staying put. I'm not budging. We'll file a petition, find a solution to get us out of this mess. Then we'll pick up our lives. We'll marry the children and receive grandchildren here, in our home. We just need a little more patience."

He spoke this way to his wife, but he didn't believe a word he was saying. Or maybe he, too, wanted to cling to one last hope before he fell victim to pain and despair.

July 22, 2019, 3:00 a.m.

Residents of neighboring buildings who hadn't received demolition orders—perhaps because they were far enough from the wall not to threaten "state security"—gathered around the family that had become the object of everyone's pity. Umm Muhammad was pleading for help from the Lord. But she couldn't detect even the slightest glimmer of humanity in the soldiers who stood hemming her in with her children and husband. Abu Muhammad had slumped to the ground, and with him fell his tears, announcing the beginning of his inward defeat. The towering, sturdy man who had resisted for the sake of his dream, his cause, his very existence—even this pillar of strength had fallen to the ground.

He was surrounded by soldiers armed with rifles, machine guns, and bombs, ready to destroy everything around them. As for Abu Muhammad, he was armed with nothing but tears. He covered his eyes with his arm, but couldn't suppress his groans.

The neighbors were in a rage over the callous treatment they'd endured at the hands of the soldiers, who cursed and beat anyone who came near them or Abu Muhammad. Not satisfied with displacing them in the dead of night, the soldiers wanted these people to be thoroughly humiliated.

After all the soldiers' provocations—the insults, the pushing and beating of women, elders, even children—things were about to get violent. Young men began to clash with the troops, risking arrest. Suddenly, however, a man in the crowd started trying to defuse the situation. In a stentorian voice, he attempted to shed light on the condition of the man who had collapsed on the ground. The agitated young men backed down, exhibiting a patience whose source they couldn't identify. Maybe God had granted them a serenity they would need to bear what was coming.

Six years earlier
Abu Muhammad, fifty years old, had spent his life repairing cars and changing spare parts. Umm Muhammad was the model wife his mother had chosen for him.

Abu Muhammad returned to their rented apartment in the Jabel Mukaber area, which could no longer accommodate him and his growing family. He'd started searching around a year earlier for a house in Jerusalem. He'd traveled all over the suburbs to find the right place. Since childhood, his dream had been to own a house where he could bring his mother and father, his brothers and their families. But his parents had passed before he even started realizing this dream, and his brothers had found homes of their own. Still, he hoped to give his wife and children their own nest.

One day, at last, he found a suitable place. It was quiet, and to his amazement the price was just slightly over his life savings—the money he'd been stashing since he was sixteen. He hurried back to tell Umm Muhammad about it.

"I've found a great apartment," he announced excitedly. "It's in a good area, still under construction. Its price is reasonable, so we can manage if we cut back on expenses until we've made the first payment. Then we'll have our own home!"

"Where did you find it?" she asked.

"In Wadi Hummus—Sur Baher."

"Isn't that part of the West Bank? Didn't we agree we'd buy a house in Jerusalem?"

"It actually *is* in Jerusalem, just not listed as such. It's a long story. But come with me now so I can show it to you."

On the way, he explained to her that the apartment was located where the neighborhoods of Wadi Hummus,

Deir al-Amoud, and al-Muntar met, to the southeast of Jerusalem, an area that belonged to the village of Sur Baher. These neighborhoods weren't included within the occupation municipality in Jerusalem in 1967, making them part of the West Bank.

As the separation wall was being constructed during the Second Intifada, it was supposed to run along the Israeli municipal borders of Jerusalem. In other words, it was supposed to separate "Jerusalem lands" (under the authority of the municipality) from "West Bank lands." As it turned out, however, land on both sides of the wall belonged to Sur Baher, which meant splitting families. Consequently, people protested the proposed path of the wall, and their petition succeeded in getting the wall shifted over to the east. There thus came to be two classifications for the West Bank: West Bank territories inside the wall (that is, on the Palestinian side), and West Bank territories outside the wall (that is, on the Israeli side—the Jerusalem side).

July 22, 2019, 4:00 a.m.
The Israeli occupation army cordoned off Wadi Hummus, closed all entrances and exits through adjacent neighborhoods and the road to Sur Baher, and declared it a closed military zone.

"Where are you going? This is a closed military zone."

"I live in this building and I want to check on my wife and children. We all live in these buildings, and we need to be able to get home."

"Those are the orders."

Like automatons, the soldiers didn't see, hear, or comprehend—they just followed orders. They couldn't have cared less if those orders would bring down homes, destroy livelihoods and dreams, or deprive entire families of vital resources for hours or days on end.

The man with the thunderous voice tried again to stand up to this provocation. Unintimidated by the soldiers' weapons or orders, he shouted his demand that the people be allowed to cross the street to check on their wives and children. He continued raising his voice to make sure he was being heard by someone of higher rank than the soldier-robot in front of him. And, in fact, it was a higher-ranking officer who relented and permitted the crowd to disperse toward their homes, in exchange for their cooperating to get things done as quickly and efficiently as possible.

In a burst of quasi humanity, the officer "allowed" them to reach their homes. But before this, he had them line up to tell him exactly which building each of them was going back to. He also told those with cars to remove them from a small building being used as a parking garage, so it could be demolished.

Meanwhile, several journalists arrived. Some risked their lives running down back roads and hidden alleys to reach rooftops where they could film the events taking place.

Twenty-five years earlier
Dalal—Umm Muhammad—had just finished her high school exams when Umm Hassan met her at a wedding and soon chose her to be her son's wife. After asking about

the girl's family, Umm Hassan had asked them for her hand on behalf of her son Hassan—Abu Muhammad—even before telling him about it. This was how marriage worked in those days. As for Dalal, she'd had another future in mind: she would be the first girl in her family to graduate from university. She hadn't really thought about what she would study, though she was leaning toward being a teacher, like Najwa, who taught her Arabic at school.

When the request came for Dalal to marry Hassan, her father thought it would be best for her, especially since the groom was from a respectable family. He knew nothing about Dalal's dreams, of course, and even if he had, he might not have approved of them. In any case, he agreed to the proposal and so did she. In so doing, Dalal postponed her dreams and ambitions indefinitely. Or rather, she transferred them to her future children—her new hope was to have a daughter who would fulfill those dreams in her stead.

July 22, 2019, 5:00 a.m.
He hurriedly climbed the steps that led to his house, which held his wife, his children, and everything he owned—the home that gave him a sense of security. Once inside, he shed tears of grief and helplessness, drawing strength from his children's innocent eyes and his wife's warm embrace.

"Tell me what's happening down there," Umm Muhammad said.

"What's happening is injustice, oppression, humiliation, pain. We stood idly by with locks on our mouths while a proud man's spirit was broken. He collapsed on the ground. Weapons and bulldozers demolished their homes before their very eyes."

"Put your trust in God. He's the one who will give us justice. Don't let on that you feel oppressed or helpless. Instead, stand tall and never back down. Declare your rage to the end, and help however you can."

"I will. I swear I will. Anyway, I came now to tell you that they're going to demolish that small building next to ours. Watch out for the kids and close the windows. Keep water on hand in case any of them chokes on the dust, the gunpowder, or the tear gas. And if you need anything, scream, and I'll come right away."

"Take care of yourself. Be well, and stay strong."

July 22, 2019, 7:00 a.m.

After they'd demolished the parking garage and the army had evacuated the residential buildings, they demolished those too, one after another. The bulldozers and excavators ran back and forth, destroying long years' worth of toil in mere minutes. In the process, they crushed the spirits of men who had supported their families by the sweat of their brow, and who sat along the roadside weeping, their mustaches wet with tears. They'd been helpless to save their modest toehold in this mighty city. The space where they'd found refuge for so long now seemed like nothing but a bubble that had burst at the first sting of these metallic yellow scorpions.

Some soldiers took selfies in front of the demolished buildings to document their "achievements."

July 22, 2019, 9:00 a.m.

The officers and soldiers prepared to blow up the building that was still under construction. The plan was to plant explosives on all the floors that were in violation of the law, as the building consisted of eight floors, four of which threatened "state security." The commander of the unit ordered his men to enter a nearby building to distribute warning leaflets. They wanted to storm homes to alert women and children about how they were going to "preserve residents' safety."

If it hadn't been for the men who confronted the soldiers at the entrance to the building and prevented them from all going in, the day's list of crimes would have been a lot longer. The man with the loud voice stipulated that only two soldiers be allowed to accompany each officer, and that they be escorted by residents to each house. After a series of skirmishes and shouting matches with the residents, the unit commander reluctantly agreed to their demands. Then they distributed the leaflets—their way of absolving the army of consequences.

July 22, 2019, 10:00 a.m.

After rising "early" that morning, men in suits accustomed to media appearances sipped coffee and browsed the news and social media. As they ate their breakfasts, changed their clothes, or stood in their mirrors straightening their ties, they took note of the happenings in Wadi Hummus. After swinging by the newspaper vendor, and perhaps the barber, they "rushed" to the scene, only to discover that a curfew had been imposed, and that no one was allowed to enter or exit the demolition sites. So they stood on the outskirts, in front of TV cameras, spouting condemnations of the ongoing events. Then, with clear consciences now that they'd done their duty toward their people, they took off for their homes while families slept on sidewalks.

July 22, 2019, 1:00 p.m.

Hope is always born out of the womb of suffering. The situation in Wadi Hummus was crueler than mere suffering, and a new life was being birthed—out of the womb of a woman in the building opposite the one where the explosives had been planted.

Is fate toying with us? It's a question that comes to mind in situations like this. Couldn't this child have decided to come on some day other than this one? A day of demolition, displacement, and pain, and most importantly in his case, a day when the neighborhood had been declared a closed military zone? Obviously a stubborn kid was on his way into the world.

"My wife's going into labor! We've got to get her to the hospital right away! The baby will die in her womb unless we get her out of here, now!"

"What do we do? How are we going to get her out under this curfew?"

"We'll try . . . We'll try to talk to one of the soldiers. Come with me . . ."

"Listen, sir, we have an emergency here. A woman's gone into labor, and we need to get her to the hospital ASAP."

"No one's allowed out of this military zone."

"Can't you hear me? The woman is pregnant! And if we don't get her to the hospital now, the baby will die, and she might die too."

"The orders I have say no exit or entry."

"To hell with your orders! My wife's going to die . . . Listen, sir: Speak to your commander. Tell him we either need to get an ambulance, or let her husband take her in his car. This is a matter of life and death . . . Try to understand us."

The soldier stood there robot-like, neither blinking nor looking them in the eye. He once again recited the phrases that had been drilled into him. Then he fell silent. He had no answers. He couldn't think. He seemed to have no sense of those around him, or even of his own humanity. He just stood stiffly, gripping his gun in anticipation of any sudden movement. Like a fighter standing motionless on a battlefield, he showed no concern for the lives that might be lost if he failed to act.

The only solution they could find was to keep shouting as loudly as they could in the hope of making themselves heard to someone higher in rank, someone who would respond based on logic rather than mechanical commands. And at last that happened.

"What's all the commotion?"

"They claim there's a woman in labor and they want to take her to the hospital."

"Where is she?"

"She's at home, and if we don't move her now, she and the baby might both die!"

"I'll look into whether the request can be approved."

"*What?* Time is running out, and you're killing her!"

"I told you I'll look into it."

In reality, this officer had the authority to approve or reject the request. All he wanted was to pile new insults and humiliations atop the ones he'd already inflicted on entire families.

The officer watched them from a distance through his sunglasses, alternately laughing and feigning seriousness while his victims renewed their determination to wait in silence. The display only ended when the officer saw the look of brokenness in the husband's eyes. Once this victory had been scored, he called the man over and gestured to him to bring his wife.

"You've got ten minutes to get out of here. If you don't leave before they're up, you've lost your chance. Now don't waste our time."

July 22, 2019, 7:00 p.m.

Over the last few hours, the occupation army had been busy planting explosives all over the building, and stressing to the area's residents that they should open their windows to keep them from shattering.

At zero hour, the soldiers stood some distance away with a detonator. They prepared to document their achievement on video, then pressed a button and blew up the building. With it, they killed its owner's source of livelihood, and the life savings and dreams of countless buyers.

From the top of the hill, they congratulated themselves, shaking hands, hugging, smiling.

Meanwhile, on the top floor of the building opposite the target, people had gathered to document the blast with pained prayers and shouts of "Allahu Akbar!" They cursed those standing on the hilltop.

When the building exploded, colossal quantities of dust and debris came flying. The neighbors panicked. "Close the windows!" many shouted. The army's instructions to open the windows had been a ruse. Rubble shot out to the adjacent building and a cloud began spreading throughout the apartments on both sides.

Her eighteen-month-old son on her heels and a newborn in her arms, a mother ran to close the windows of her house before she and her children suffocated or were hit by flying debris. Choking, she placed her baby on the sofa.

Her husband rushed down from the upper floor and gasped. "Grab the boy and get out now! Stay at the neighbor's until the dust has cleared a little. Come on!"

"No, you take him! Zain's on the sofa. Hurry and I'll catch up with you."

Charging through the dust and debris that occupied her home just as oppression had occupied her city, she snatched her baby, then exited without a glance at anything in the house, her only concern being to make sure her family was safe.

July 22, 2019, 8:00 p.m.
After carrying out their mission, the soldiers gathered up their equipment, their bulldozers, their cars, and all their other tools of humiliation, leaving one hundred homes in ruins.

In an extraordinary city, with all that goes against the ordinary, and against us personally, all we could do was weep, stumble around, and chant slogans. We could only respond to the extraordinary with the ordinary. Similarly, the man who had fainted had done all he could in the face of the yellow scorpions, the rubble, the displacement, the heartbreak, and the fear. And as soon as he came out of his swoon, he would find his oppressors ready to devour yet more of what was precious to him.

Is ten minutes enough? And what exactly is it enough for? To cry? To scream? To make a heroic decision? To say goodbye to one's dreams, and the nail one managed to drive into a tiny part of this city? Or even to gather up one's disappointment from the various corners of the house? Is ten minutes really enough for anybody to face all this?

Tell me now: What's the difference between demolition, displacement, and humiliation in Wadi Hummus on July 22, 2019, and demolition, displacement, and the occupation of the village of Lajjun on April 15, 1948? What's the difference between the Nakba of 1948 and the Nakba of Wadi Hummus in 2019?

July 22, 2019, 2:30 a.m.: "You've got ten minutes to vacate the house. Once the ten minutes are up, we'll destroy it and everything inside, even you!"

July 21, 2019: All petitions demanding postponement of the demolition on various grounds are denied.

June 18, 2019: "You have one month to demolish these buildings. Otherwise, we'll demolish them ourselves."

June 11, 2019: The Supreme Court denies the residents' petition against the demolition decrees, and rejects alternative solutions such as raising the wall in that area and installing surveillance cameras.

2015: Owners of homes and buildings in Wadi Hummus, in the vicinity of the separation wall, receive demolition orders from the occupation army.

2011: Military Resolution No. 11/08/AB prohibits construction on either side of the wall within a distance of one hundred to three hundred meters, depending on the area.

2002: The separation wall is constructed during the Second Intifada.

1993: After the Oslo Accords are signed, Wadi Hummus, Deir al-Amoud, and al-Muntar are given different classifications—(A), (B), and (C)—which overlap to some extent.

April 15, 1948: The village of Lajjun, located at the point where the western edge of Marj ibn Amer meets the Carmel mountain range, is overtaken and demolished in preparation for the construction of the Megiddo kibbutz.

Time: Is it taking us forward, carrying us back, or merely repeating itself?

FLEEING FROM THE ASSYRIAN SOLDIERS

BY ZIAD KHADASH

Alleys of Ancient Jerusalem

Translated by Catherine Cobham

E very time I set foot in this city, I risk being abducted. God, it's the same vision: a woman waiting for me. She may have come and gone because I was late, held up at Israeli checkpoints. She may turn up in a little while, since I arrived early. She may be dead and buried because I fantasized about her. She may be here but angry, not wanting to see me, because I let her down by dying. She may have made a deal with one of this city's narrow alleys and swapped roles with it and become an alleyway herself, where vendors' handcarts, believers, soldiers, and lovers jostle one another as they hurry along, while the alleyway becomes a woman overflowing with rivers of elusive desires. The alley yearns for desires, the woman for memories. Every time I go down to Jerusalem—and I don't know why I think the road from Ramallah to Jerusalem goes "down"—I sense that holiness is merely the sister of sin; that the temples, monasteries, old streets, graves, and tombs only acquire their dignity, heavenly meaning, and depth in the presence of a woman; and that femininity only grows more magical and mysterious and obscure in the presence of legends and temples.

Before the Second Intifada, I used to go to Jerusalem all the time, traveling its streets and history, or seeing a friend in the hospital, or visiting on a school trip. After each of these long-ago visits, I told my friends about a strange feeling I had there: someone is waiting for me, someone who loves me and will take me by the hand and roam the streets and neighborhoods with me.

If I classified Palestinian cities according to how feminine or masculine they were, Jerusalem would be far and away the most feminine: the whispers seeping from the old walls, the soft church lights on still evenings, the smooth stone steps, the reflective amble of passersby, the tears of believers before silent icons—all bring me face-to-face with a special kind of woman, fluid like time, frozen like place.

I'm in Jerusalem now. I arrived a short while ago and make my way down a dusty street out of sight of the soldiers. I risk being abducted again, but it's strange this time. I've begun to feel dizzy, the ground of Jerusalem heavy beneath my feet, my steps light. Have I started to lose my sense of things? At the Damascus Gate, I felt I was about to meet her. She told me she would be with her large family—father, mother, grandmother, grandfather, brothers, sisters, uncles, and aunts—and wouldn't be able to see me easily. Now I'm walking in the alleyways as if I'm walking on human bodies, fearful, wary of treading on the laughter of a servant of the king of Salem, or on the memory of a victim of the siege of Jebus. I can't forget that event, as I witnessed it. I hid in a cave near the Mamilla Pool. The occupiers killed thousands of Jebusites.

They breached the wall and attacked people—children, women, men. This was stated in a manuscript that Dhat Zahira, a Palestinian writer from Ramallah, would discover thousands of years later in the tower of an old church in the Christian Quarter. He will discover it while moving in to kiss his beloved. It'll surprise him to see a piece of material protruding from a narrow crack between two large stones. He'll tug at it, and he and his sweetheart will read: "Manuscript of the monk Indicus Straitus, 614 AD." The man and woman will fall into a kind of wild daze where times are confused and places fluid. Who are they? They embrace. She bites him on the neck, he bites her little finger. They do that to return to their present, but it doesn't work. They wake up suddenly to the sound of a man weeping nearby. They descend the tower and see Jeremiah, the sad prophet, slowly walking home.

"Where are you going, sad prophet?" asks the man's beloved.

"I'm going home, my daughter, for nobody heeds my warnings. I have despaired of my people's foolishness. I said to them, *Do not rebel against the Babylonians*, but they did not take my advice. In fact, they mocked me and accused me of cowardice. So now, Nebuchadnezzar captures my people and sends them into exile in Babylon. I was with him a short time ago and he released me, saying, *Wretched are a people who defy a prophet sent by their god*."

I am still waiting for my girlfriend in Jerusalem. She calls me: "Ziad, there's only one way to do this. You have to come with a friend to rescue me from my family."

Now I'm standing in front of thousands of my people. We're celebrating the building of Jebus and its new design. I am the priest of God Most High. My name is Melchizedek, king of Salem. I have never shed anyone's blood. I have never cheated on a woman. After the celebration I will meet Abraham, who is on his way to Egypt via Jebus. I will offer him bread and wine as a gift. Jebus will remain fortified against its enemies, for I have built it on four hills: Zion, Moriah, Bezita, and Ophel. I stand with her on Mount Ophel, and she is astonished by how close our hands are to the sky. I shout at the top of my voice: "Hold your hand up in the air! Don't you feel God's hand?"

She is running between the rooms in the tower like a gazelle chasing its prey. She takes out her camera and photographs the Dome of the Rock. Jebus lies below us. We are watching a meeting in a nearby citadel: Jebus's leaders are gathered around a small rock discussing the increasingly frequent raids by the children of Israel. They are wondering whether to send a messenger to Egypt to ask the pharaoh for support.

I take her hand and we run toward the Jaffa Gate, panting. David has attacked Jebus, intending to occupy it. Everyone on the street is scrambling, panicking; thirty thousand fighters under the command of David's nephew Joab are slaughtering people and driving them from their homes. The knights of Jebus resist fiercely, but the aggressors manage to occupy Ophel, the hill overlooking the village of Siloam. Exhausted, we make our way to Ein Rogel, the spring where Jebusites draw water, only to find invaders closing it off so the people will die of thirst.

In the Church of the Holy Sepulchre, I ask her, "Do you feel a sense of awe in church like I do?" She says yes, and I ask, "Why don't we feel that in other places of worship?" She bends her head and doesn't reply.

A few days later, she calls from her faraway city to say, "The paintings on church walls tell many stories. The image and the story: there's the awe."

She rests her head on my shoulder. I kiss her lips, calm as a thief, confident that her parents aren't home. I squeeze her breast and she trembles. Suddenly Helena, mother of Emperor Constantine, enters with dozens of strong guards. We are taken aback until we see her reassuring smile. Helena asks one of her companions, "Where is the cross?" and a person called Bishop Macarius tells her that the Jews threw soil and trash on it. On her order, priests clear the garbage. Then with her own hand she takes out the fragments of three crosses and asks the bishop, "Which is the cross of the Messiah?" When he indicates the true cross, she orders the building of the Church of the Holy Sepulchre, in this very spot.

My cell phone rings. It's her: "I'm coming. Wait for me. I've run away from my family and now they're looking for me."

In shackles, we walk among thousands of captives, terrified. We are being sent into exile in Babylon along with our families. A madman called Nebuchadnezzar is taking us there as punishment for our intifada against him. Farewell, Uru-Salim—Jerusalem—city of love, massacres, and hills. Now we are descending the steps of the Jaffa Gate. She's carrying her black jacket, a blue handkerchief, a small leather handbag, a camera, and a red apple. At some point we lose our way, but some school-children direct us to the tower. All I'm carrying is my confusion. We sit down in a local café whose proprietor is amazed to see a beautiful Arab woman in a place that's only for men. She gives me a ring, I give her a pen. We take selfies. At the door of the café stands an Assyrian with harsh, strange-looking features, a fighter in the army of Shalmaneser, king of Assyria. Jerusalem is occupied again! The proprietor apologizes to us: he wants to close up shop and go home.

Battles to resist the Assyrians will break out soon. My God! Aren't the invaders tired of invading this city? My gazelle's phone rings. It's her family: "Where are you, crazy woman?" We laugh and run through the alleys of Jerusalem.

I'm still waiting for her, on my own in Jerusalem. As we climb the steps of the ancient tower, the guard tells us we only have half an hour. It's a very narrow spiral staircase. We hear a sound like an aircraft taking off. It's the wind, I tell her, as she continues the twisting ascent in silence. When we reach the top, I step back, terrified of the height. She laughs. I rush to her lips, seek protection in her curves. In the first room I lean toward her breast, take it out slowly and fearfully. She gasps and bites me on the neck, twice.

We head for the Damascus Gate and are surprised to find her family shopping. We see them but they don't see us. She is stunned and I run away. A few moments later it starts to rain heavily. I look behind me and don't see her; the heads and shoulders crowding the alleyways are blocking the view.

As I leave the tower, the guard asks me, "What's that rock you've got in your hand?"

"It's one of the many rocks that fell off the wall in front of me," I answer.

Surprised, he says: "Excuse me, sir, but some tourists said they saw you kissing the walls of the rooms and talking to yourself."

I don't respond and head on to Ramallah, fleeing from the Assyrian soldiers who have been chasing me since morning because I don't have an entry permit for Jebus. I have a silver ring on my hand and two bites on my neck.

PART II

Dreaming, Praying City

CITY OF LOVE AND LOSS

by Mahmoud Shukair
Omar Ibn al-Khattab Square

Translated by Catherine Cobham

Rain

Layla came back. She said she was hesitant about the relationship that had developed between us. She apologized. I accepted her apology and forgave her for the worry and pain she'd caused me. Layla is the daughter of rich business people; she works as a teacher at a school inside the Jerusalem wall. I fell in love with her when I got to know her by chance, and she fell in love with me, but her family is the problem.

Anyway, she came back, and we contemplated the city's houses together as we walked through the streets. Rain fell gently, knocking on the windows like a shy child, never slipping inside the houses, playing its rain game alone in the streets and squares without blaming anyone or saying anything to suggest anger.

Layla and I were enjoying the walk, paying no attention to the soldiers deployed here and there. Then we parted, hoping to meet again: in the café or in the kingdom of dreams.

Dream One

At night I saw her. We slept together after we'd made

sure the windows were firmly shut. She took refuge from the biting cold in the warmth of my body, and we didn't expect the soldiers to come.

But they turned up in our dream, and we had to follow the dream to the end. They dragged us out of bed and threw us into the street. Then they put explosives all around the house and blew it up.

"We don't have a house anymore," she said in alarm.

"I'll build a house for you," I said.

She went on sleeping and I began to build a house whose ceiling was made of roses and its walls of words.

It was a house that explosives could not touch, a house able to survive.

Dream Two

I saw her wandering through the city markets one evening. She was wearing a dress embroidered in green and red, with a kaffiyeh draped around her neck.

"What's brought you so far from home?" I asked.

"My home isn't far away." The question seemed to surprise her.

We would have disagreed over the distance, if her dream hadn't been so gentle, and mine the same. I was quick to take her hand when she held it out. It lay in my hand like a little bird. We began wandering the markets. She walked beside me, graceful as a gazelle. I was glad I'd met her by chance, without asking her on a date. Suddenly she realized the city would soon be under curfew. She was scared and clung to me so I'd protect her from the soldiers' wrath.

"Don't be afraid," I said, composed and confident, "my house is nearby."

She didn't argue, perhaps so that our dream wouldn't be wasted. We went into the house and locked the door. Her light dress suggested many possibilities.

Before I got near her, I was woken by the noise of a warplane circling above.

Her Bed

The next evening we were sitting in the café by a window overlooking the street. We could see the square, where there was a lot of activity from Israeli soldiers and settlers, and the end of the old wall, the citadel, and the tightly packed buildings that had resisted the tyranny of time. Layla felt secure because her family was spending the night in their winter house in Jericho, to enjoy the warmth away from Jerusalem's cold weather. She refused to go with them and they didn't argue, which meant that we could spend more time sitting in the café. I was happy.

As I was trying to dissect the mystery of time, the differences in people's moods, and the reasons humans move from place to place, I asked her, "What does this evening mean?" And before she could answer I continued, "There's a gentle moon and clouds, and a silent woman nearby, and delicate feelings and some ancient grief and ancient places."

She played with a strand of hair falling over her eyes. "That's how poets talk."

I didn't respond. I was looking outside, to where the

lights were coloring the shape of the place. She was look-ing out there too, letting her thoughts wander.

After a silence, she put the question back to me: "Yes, what does this evening mean?" And she began searching my eyes for an answer, while I rejoiced in the beauty of hers. Then, as if she'd remembered something, she asked, "What did your dream mean when you shut the door be-hind us and were so focused on my dress?"

The question didn't surprise me. "Don't worry," I said, "you're safe."

She was silent for a few more moments, peering in-tently at me. "Does this mean you're no use to women?" she joked.

"I hope it won't be too long before we know the an-swer to that," I replied calmly.

She was embarrassed by my words. We both laughed, then fell silent, pondering the complications surrounding our relationship. That didn't last long, perhaps because it was mentally exhausting, or perhaps because our hunt for meanings was unsuccessful for one reason or another. We began chatting uninhibitedly, and both of us felt upset when I told her about the neighbors' house, which had been blown up by soldiers a few days earlier, reduced to rubble.

We pictured the scene sorrowfully. A few moments later a group of soldiers, with a couple of female conscripts, made a surprise raid on the café and asked for our ID cards.

They examined them carefully and one of the soldiers searched me. Another, a female Ethiopian Jew, searched Layla, groping her breast with malice.

When they left, Emile said, "This isn't the first time they've burst into my café." He paused. "Sometimes they pretend to be Arabs. Once, three boys and a girl came, speaking Arabic. They sat near a group of young men and listened to their conversation, in the hopes of foiling a plot against the occupying state—merciful God! If only! They stayed in the café for half an hour or more with me watching them."

Maryam listened to her husband's bitter words. She was obviously sad—she's a sensitive, intelligent woman, with the calm kind of beauty that invites respect. "Amazing. It's really amazing," she said. "Male and female conscripts just out of high school, flaunting their uniforms and machine guns, storming into Jerusalem whenever they please to exercise their hatred here, in places that don't belong to them. Then they go back to their homes that used to belong to Palestinians in Jerusalem and Lod, Ramla, Beersheba, Ashkelon, Jaffa, Haifa, and Acre, to boast to their mothers about the number of Palestinians they've shot or wounded."

Emile nodded his head, contemplating his wife's lovely face. Layla and I stayed silent.

Soon we left the café and headed down the street. When I opened the car door for Layla, she thanked me and got in. Her question about me looking at her flimsy dress in our dream was still rolling around in my head. I tried my best to blank it. We made our way to Beit Hanina al-Jadida. The houses crammed together on both sides of the street, the light cascading from windows and balconies, suggested some sort of stability.

As we approached Layla's house, I was overwhelmed by a desire to know its inside, to put an end to the terror that came over me whenever I found myself near it. It was unlit, but its shape was visible in the streetlights. It had an unmistakably dignified aura. I expressed my desire hesitantly.

"I don't mind," said Layla, "but the house is surrounded by cameras."

That was reason enough not to proceed, and anyway I was no longer so keen to enter, as Layla's question had started to rattle around in my head again.

But before she got out of the car, she said, "Wait while I disable the cameras."

A few minutes later she appeared at a window and beckoned me. I approached the house, eager, unable to hide my emotion, and passed through the well-fortified door, prey to many different feelings. Layla and I were alone in the vast house. She took me on a tour and I was dazzled by the beauty of the chandeliers, the paintings on the walls, and the crystal figurines of rabbits, cats, monkeys, dogs, and horses spread throughout the living room— as well as the crystal goblets elegantly arranged on the ebony buffet, and the large beds and luxurious wardrobes.

From the door of her bedroom, I could see her bed, her closet, her clothes and shoes scattered about, and posters covering the walls—of Fairuz, Rim Banna, Macadi Nahhas, Ammar Hassan, Abeer Sansour, Mohammed Assaf, Yacoub Shaheen, and other contemporary singers. From the high ceiling hung yet another chandelier; on a table sat notebooks, a computer, pens, and papers. There was a handbag on a leather armchair, a pink nightdress draped over the end of the bed, and wooden shelves fixed to the wall, where poetry collections, novels, and other books were arranged in neat rows. A whole life in all its splendor. Layla stood beside me, smiling.

"Do you like my room in spite of the mess?" she inquired coquettishly.

"I like it very much," I said, "and I even like the mess."

Then I was gripped by a desire to take a few more steps into the room and lie down on her bed so that I might leave a trace of myself there, and perhaps take a trace of her with me. I hesitated and she remained silent, the same smile still on her lips.

(When he told me about this later, I said to him, "If only you had lain in my bed, then I would have seen you there every night. You deny yourself even this simple pleasure, Qays the madman!* Qays the idiot!" He struck his forehead with the palm of his hand and said, "Next time I will lie in your bed and stay there till morning.")

She offered me a coffee. I declined, not wanting to stay any longer, and headed for the door.

That night I didn't sleep as I floated in delicious daydreams: Layla was at the heart of them all.

To Jaffa

We had agreed to go to Jaffa.

She was waiting on the sidewalk for me. The weather was mild, the sun disappearing and reappearing among

---

*A reference to the traditional Arab love story of Qays and Layla, to which the current tale alludes. Qays is also known as Majnun Layla—"Layla's Madman."

the clouds. The traffic was constant on the road linking Jerusalem with Jaffa.

"I love going to Jaffa and the sea there," I said. "I can be closer to your roots."

"Yes," she responded, sitting beside me in the car, "we're going to the place where my ancestors lived."

I complimented her on her pink dress.

"Shut up, shut up," she teased, imitating her father when he didn't like what someone said.

She fell silent as Fairuz's voice rang out from the radio: *"Oh vines of El Alaly, your grapes belong to us. My beautiful, my precious, how I love you."*

Layla's feelings poured out and overflowed like the glistening waters of a stream. She unfastened her seat belt. Shaking her hips and thrusting her chest out, she snapped her fingers and sang along with Fairuz. I couldn't join her, so I kept tapping on the steering wheel with a sort of rhythm.

We arrived in Jaffa and walked through the streets among Jewish men and women. Ambiguous streets, betraying the fact that the place had been forcibly removed from its original identity. A light breeze played with Layla's hair and the hem of her dress.

We approached her grandfather's old house. It had high windows and arches.

"I visited this house many times with my family," she said. "Now there's a Jewish family here. They came from Poland, and wouldn't let us enter, not even once. We had to be content with looking at it from the outside.

"Like other people from the city," she went on, "my

grandfather was forced to leave everything behind—places from his childhood, the land, trees, houses, furniture, books, and shops—because of the bullets that rained down, killing innocent people.

"He came to Jerusalem and the fighting there led to the city being divided. He settled in the eastern part, and always missed the sea and the smells of it carried by the winds in Jaffa. There was no sea in Jerusalem, not much water at all. Even though Jerusalem had a certain status in his eyes, Jaffa was always his dream. Its sea filled his memory.

"He set up a business in the Musrara neighborhood to sell wheat and flour, and owned other shops inside the city wall. He continued his life with his family, patiently rebuilding what he had lost. Trade was in every pore of his body; he never gave it up and bequeathed it to his children. My father," she concluded, "was born in Jerusalem soon after the Nakba in 1948."

We walked through the streets of Jaffa, looking to our right and left as if we had never been there before.

"Jaffa was a female city first and foremost," Layla said. "All contradictions coexisted in it. And like Haifa and Acre and Alexandria and Beirut, it was a city of the sea. It welcomed all the ideas, arts, fashions, and eccentric innovations the sea brought. Its inhabitants devoured every new thing with open minds. They talked, as they sat in cafés and bars, about the danger surrounding the city, and in moments of enlightenment about the charms of female dancers in the nightclubs. The city was not happy with the contraband weapons and immigrants the sea threw at it."

We mourned one of the most beautiful cities of Palestine, which Layla's forefathers had called the Bride of the Sea. Then we set off together for the shore.

She walked beside me on the sand, barefoot. I was barefoot too. She hitched up her dress as if preparing to plunge into the water, which was only a few steps away. The sea was vast and boundless, inviting us to cast off our cares. In its presence, the hint of sadness on Layla's face didn't last long. She moved so gracefully.

We came to a spot on the shore where there were fewer people. She began to undress, shyly, and I lowered my eyes, suppressing a sudden rush of feeling. The waters crashed to the shore and the waves rose, perhaps in celebration of her body, perhaps for some other reason. She put on a bathing suit that covered her chest, stomach, and thighs. While she stuffed her clothes into her bag, I turned away, undressed quickly, and pulled on my swimming trunks.

I took her hand and led her toward the water. She seemed timid and I reassured her, saying I was an excellent swimmer and she shouldn't be afraid. She grieved for the sandcastles she used to build at the seaside. Her grandfather and other men from earlier generations of the family had been good swimmers when they lived here, or so her grandmother used to tell her when they sat up talking at night. I told her I learned to swim in the pools of Jerusalem.

I swam and she watched me apprehensively. I returned to her and saw the water was barely up to the bottom of her thighs. I lifted her in my arms and encouraged her to move her limbs in the water. She beat her arms and legs on the surface, but was still afraid.

She cowered against me whenever a wave hit her, and I protected her from the onslaught. I was certain that my life without her would be nothing.

Without her my house would be empty, devoid of warmth, meaningless.

Chains

One day, Layla and I were at the military checkpoint on the way from Ramallah to Jerusalem. We'd already waited three hours.

We drank coffee from a street vendor, exchanged the latest news of the city, and refrained from complaining about the intense heat, even though we were exhausted. Layla said her bladder was about to burst, and there were no toilets around.

"If they believed in peace," I said, "they wouldn't have put a checkpoint here. For over fifty years they've been here, tormenting us. Unfortunately, the Jews who are sympathetic to us, the peace lovers, are a minority, helpless in the face of the rising right-wing extremism."

Next to us was a woman who appeared indifferent to the soldiers' arrogance, brushing her hair gracefully as if she was getting ready for bed.

The crush was at its worst: men, women, and children all waiting for permission to go through. The soldiers standing behind the barrier, clutching their rifles, looked weary, as if *we* were detaining *them*.

Confusion

Another day Layla and I were in the car with the June sun blazing down on us.

She seemed somewhat confused. She sank down into the seat and put her sunglasses on. Without waiting for me to ask, she said she was being questioned by her father and brothers about why she got home late some days, especially as she was on her summer vacation now.

"They keep playing the same old record," she said, "a lot of questions accompanied by sighs of anger and annoyance, and fear for our reputation and honor."

She said her family's resentment toward her had grown after a thirty-five-year-old engineer came to them wanting to marry her. When they asked her opinion, she refused him on the pretext that he was eleven years older than her. They were unconvinced, saying she was crazy for turning away an engineer any girl would want.

"I put up with their hurtful words," she said, "and continued to reject the man. I had to make up reasons why I was late coming home. I would hide in my room, asking myself, *What if they knew we meet up in a café near the Jaffa Gate, or that we go to the seaside in Jaffa and the countryside around Jerusalem, and to Ramallah?* If my father knew that, he'd have a stroke, and if my brothers knew, their blood pressure would soar and they'd probably kill someone." She paused. "I feel ashamed of myself because I'm forced to lie."

I was driving without paying much attention to the road as I listened to her. She spoke nonstop and I only uttered a few words.

When we arrived in the countryside, the sun was ripening the wheat planted some distance away from an Israeli settlement. Maybe the workers were late harvesting it for some reason. Thinking about why it was still there when it was a ripe yellow aroused many emotions in me, perhaps in Layla too.

We walked slowly, careful not to brush against the wheat, until we came to a smooth rock overlooking a deep valley. We sat there, letting our legs dangle over the side. Mine were close to hers and it felt intimate. I told her that we should shout so that the valley and surrounding mountains would echo our cries.

"You first!" she said with a smile.

"Laylaaaaaaa!" I shouted.

Laylaaaaaaa! the valley called back.

"Qayyyyyyys!" shouted Layla.

And the valley replied, *Qayyyyyyys!*

We repeated our cries many times, releasing pent-up energy. I noticed how pale she was.

"I'm to blame for a lot of your pain," I said.

She looked at me. "It's not your fault."

Then we fell silent.

A Third Time

I went to see Layla's family for the third time.

The first time, we went in a group of men and women. The women from my family sat with the women of the house in an inner room, and we men sat in the main room, which was amply furnished with comfortable armchairs, thick carpets, and silk curtains hanging majestically at the windows. We did not receive a friendly reception from Layla's family.

The second time, it was just me, my father, and my mother. We sat in the living room. Layla's father entered with a scowl on his face. We did not receive a friendly reception from him or her brothers.

The third time, I went alone. I was serious in my request, insistent, and it was as if I were speaking the words of Majnun Layla, "Layla's Madman," Qays Ibn al-Mulawwah:

*How can I find my way to Layla now that she wears
a veil
My dedication to her is from a time when she was still
unveiled*

Her family rejected me because I wasn't fit to be related to them by marriage—as though we were characters in some traditional Arab love poem. Moreover, they considered my coming to their house in this way an insult, a challenge that diminished their status.

I said I hoped they would change their mind: I would find a better, more distinguished job. They ridiculed me, unconvinced. Then they blamed Layla, who had rebelled against traditional principles, refused marriage to an engineer, and now wished to marry a taxi driver.

When they realized I was still determined to become part of their family, they threw me out of the house and beat me up. Two of them held me down near the garden wall while her brother pummeled me. "Do you want me to lock you in the basement?" he barked.

He repeated his threat three times. I didn't answer. They took turns thrashing me, and when their hands were tired, they stopped and told me to never return.

Layla cried through it all. From a window overlooking the garden, she yelled loud enough for her parents and the neighbors to hear: "I will never get married, except to Qays!"

A Meeting

Seven hours later she turned up, at midnight, barefoot. I was about to leave the parking lot in front of the Jerusalem wall to go home. Her hair fell over her shoulders in an endearing mess, and her lilac dress was disheveled, revealing much of her legs and arms. She ran to me. "Take me to the countryside," she said.

I was astonished at her showing up this late. I started the engine and we drove off. The weather was pleasant, the air refreshingly moist. Above us, the bright moon. The journey only took a few minutes. Lights from the Israeli settlements shone all around, and dogs barked intermittently.

"The settlers will kill us," I said.

"Don't be afraid," she said.

We left the car to go to the spot where my ancestors once lived herding sheep. Here they slept with their women, who bore children continually, and here the women washed those children under the sun. Here my ancestors received their guests. Here they betrothed the girls to the boys; here they left their abayas and swords and horses, and died. They died after begetting many sons and daughters.

We kept walking and passed near the grave of a martyr killed by the English decades ago. We could hear a distant wolf howling and jackals crying like wailing mothers. Layla looked around as if she had a plan in mind. She took off her dress and her body was like a tall palm tree. She spread the dress on the ground near the grave. Her black camisole was pulled up over her thighs. She lay down on the dress and whispered frantically, "Come on, lie on me."

"Your brother will kill you," I said.

"Don't worry. Lie on me right now."

She held out her hand and pulled me to her, unbuttoning my shirt.

I took off her camisole and moved on top of her. "You're my horse," I said.

This excited her and she mounted me, saying, "Now you're *my* horse."

We fell into a delicious trance, unconcerned with the distant howling and the creatures around us searching for food.

We clung to each other and rolled this way and that, and the sound of her sighs filled the countryside. I was pouring out the feelings that had been trapped inside me for months, and soon the tank burst and flooded her body. Crimson blood flowed from her, wetting her lilac dress.

"Are we in a dream or is this real?" she gasped.

"What's the difference? There's no difference."

She rested her head on my chest and was silent for a while. Then she spoke: "Now I can hear the ships laden with goods for my ancestors the merchants. The ships are approaching the port of Jaffa and Jaffa is opening its heart and arms and body so they can unload their cargo. Jaffa isn't only a city, she's a lustful woman who loves men."

"Now I can hear the sound of my ancestors' horses thundering over the land," I said, "and my ancestors spur them on, while the women trill with joy and raise their voices in song."

"This is our night," she said.

"Yes. Our night of nights."

Still resting her head on my chest, she told me about her great-grandfather who had fallen in love with a British tourist visiting Jaffa. Because she refused his advances, he offered to marry her and she accepted. He spent the wedding night with her in a hotel near the sea, and at dawn he took her to the hospital to stop the bleeding he had caused. Their marriage only lasted a few months. His friends teased him about the bleeding incident: "That night, you declared war on the British Mandate weighing down the country's soul." He didn't find their joke funny. Regretfully, he attributed his rough lovemaking to his excessive eagerness and uncontrollable passion.

I told her about my great-grandfather who returned to the Jerusalem countryside after a long journey. He came home after midnight, when everyone in the family was asleep. He tethered his horse in front of the hair tent, put down barley for her, and stroked her neck so she wouldn't neigh and cause trouble. His wife woke up and welcomed him with open arms. He didn't give her time to lie on the bed; he made her take hold of the tent pole. She bent over and he leaned into her doggy style and began fucking her in a frenzy. The pole shook violently, as did the whole tent. This provoked the horse, who raised her head and neighed long and loud, which in turn disturbed the dogs sleeping around the tent and made them bark until the shaking stopped.

Layla listened intently to my story about my great-grandfather and then mounted me again, blazing with passion.

At the last moment, we saw him. Layla didn't know him but I recognized him immediately. "He's the hedgehog," I told her, "a member of my family. His name is Abd al-Rahman."

He was crouched near us, watching us curiously. He put his head down right then and closed his eyes as if he couldn't see us. We didn't pay any more attention to him, as we were about to leave our dream.

A Decision

In the morning, Layla made a decision. (Yes, I made my decision, and said to myself, *My life is no more precious than the lives of prisoners who resist the occupiers on empty stomachs*. I remembered a group of them who'd spent a month or more on hunger strike. I didn't go to the breakfast table. My father noticed I wasn't there and was sullen and bad tempered. Trying to absorb some of his anger, my mother said, "Layla's ill." He believed her, but remained skeptical.)

A week passed and Layla was still on hunger strike. Her family took her to the hospital, but she wouldn't back down.

Her father feared the media attention and the headlines he could foresee in the press: "Teacher Forbidden to Marry Lover on Hunger Strike." "Prisoners in Occupiers' Jails an Inspiration: A New Way to Confront Stubborn Fathers." He visited her in the hospital and promised to let her marry whomever she wished.

She left the hospital and returned to her parents' house, weak and emaciated.

I married her three weeks later.

Morning Coffee

A month after our marriage we were having our morning coffee on our balcony. We were feeling reassured: we had gotten what we wanted and hadn't been defeated by the power of business or conventional attitudes. We knew our love story was the straightforward kind that only concerned us, nobody else. It would leave no trace, unlike the love stories we read about in books—those of Romeo and Juliet or Qays Ibn al-Mulawwah and Layla al-Aamiriya, for example. All the same, our story—every detail, bitter or sweet—would always be significant to us.

Our peace of mind did not last long: "They blew up the house of the martyr's family," a neighbor breathlessly informed us. "The martyr, the young man who killed one soldier and wounded another. Now the house is a heap of metal and stones and dust."

Layla and I looked at one another. "Not a day goes by without surprises in this country," she said. The same thought was going through my head. We agreed that we were used to surprises by now, and had no choice but to get on with our lives.

We dressed hurriedly. The heat of summer was announcing itself with ferocity. I wore shoes without socks, Layla gray jeans and a white shirt. We walked down the street, now and then picking up the pace to make sure we arrived in time. Soldiers barred our way as we approached. There was already a crowd of people blocked from proceeding.

We stood there with the others, shouting in protest against the unjust punishment that affected a whole family.

Layla had a sudden dizzy spell. I put my arm round her and we went home.

A Question

As we sat watching the news on television that evening, Layla asked, "Why can't we enjoy periods of calm like other people in the world?"

I tried to sound mature and wise: "We'll get there. One day we'll get there." Then, embarrassed by my attempt to sound knowledgeable, I repeated the question back to her: "Yes, why can't we have periods of calm?"

"If I knew, I wouldn't have asked you the question."

I still needed to show her that I was as far from being arrogant as the earth is from the sky. She rested her head on my shoulder, making me feel less awkward, and told me to stop trying to explain myself. Then we had lunch to the sound of aircraft invading our skies to let us know they were there.

When the noise abated, I said, "The issue isn't really so complicated, despite the complications surrounding it.

We have land, houses, memories, graveyards, and balconies. We forget ourselves if we forget them."

She squeezed my hand, repeating my words in a heartfelt whisper: "We forget ourselves if we forget them."

Jerusalem was on our minds in those moments, and we were as taut with emotion as two violin strings.

A Dress

The next day, Layla went to Souk el-Attarine, visiting all the clothing stalls until she decided on a multicolored print dress.

In the evening, she couldn't wait for me to rest after such a long day. She began undoing the shiny wrapping around the dress while I looked on curiously. *Everything Layla does is worth watching*, I thought. *She's a fascinating woman.*

She took off the dress and her camisole rode up above her navel, perhaps by chance, or maybe she meant to arouse me. A shiver ran through me at the sight of her body in its beguiling paleness and her panties the color of red anemones. She picked up the new dress tenderly and slipped it on. Then she stood in front of the mirror, awaiting my opinion.

"It's as beautiful as the woman wearing it," I said.

She walked toward me, the dress swaying around her body, and kissed me.

"It's true," I teased. "It falls below your knees and adds a touch of dignity to your beauty, but it's loose, and the wind might blow it up and expose your thighs as you walk down the street."

She paraded before me elegantly, as if she had antici-
pated this moment and rehearsed. She gathered the dress
around her thighs. "I'll hold it tight like this and not let
it get away."

We both laughed, then she took the dress off.

Water

We were in autumn, in the twilight, in our little house, in
the neighborhood where contradictions coexisted, sometimes disregarded, other times causing strife, and where
surprises happened.

As the people in the neighborhood were oblivious to
us, and Layla and I to them, and the birds returned ea-
gerly to their nests, in those moments when people felt
fragile and uncertain, Layla walked barefoot on the tiles,
her hair covering her naked shoulders, and said nothing.

She turned on the music and danced to its melancholy
notes. I remembered the Night of Fire that my grandmother spoke about, the night when men and women
danced in the big square in front of their houses. Seven
marriages took place on one night, in primitive rituals
borrowed from a remote past that revolved around celebrating women's bodies, begetting children, and clinging
to life's pleasures.

Now Layla danced alone, observing the rituals of the
present, which had its fair share of killing and destruction, despite its achievements and advanced culture. I was
ashamed of myself because I couldn't dance. *I'll learn to
dance*, I told myself. *Layla will teach me what I don't know,
if not this month then next month.*

I watched her, enraptured. Her pink camisole was hitched up, showing off the contours of her body, and sweat appeared on her forehead, chest, belly, and legs.

She peeled off her camisole and panties, and was desperate for water. Our water was cut off that evening.

And that was by no means a random occurrence.

AN ASTRONAUT IN JERUSALEM

BY Iyad Shamasnah

Jabel Mukaber

Translated by Roger Allen

"I want to be an astronaut, Father," the nine-year-old boy said. He was ready to go to the Rashidiya School, near Herod's Gate.

His father ignored him and bit his lip. "Come on, boy," he said, hurrying his son along. "You're gonna be late . . ." He was the last person who would want to go to space. Especially not on Saturday, his day off from the hard labor he had to do as a crane operator, smashing rocks in the settlements.

"I want to be a spaceman, Father. Why don't you listen? Our teacher told us we have to decide what we want to be when we grow up."

"Okay, you can be a driver, a doctor, an engineer . . . But a *spaceman*? Impossible! What made you think of that?"

"But don't we have space?"

"No space, no water, no air. Nothing. Everything's been stolen from us. It's all been stolen, my son."

Years earlier, what remained of Jerusalem, the Old City, the West Bank, and the Jordan Valley had all faded under occupation. Soldiers ran through the streets with an upside-down picture of the king who had previously been called "the venerable monarch." Abu al-Abd threw a photo of Nasser on the ground and crushed it. Jerusalem International Airport was now called Atarot Airport, and Lod Airport had already been renamed. Direct transport connections with Jordan came to a halt. Previously, the bus would leave the Damascus Gate for Amman in the morning and return in the evening. In those days, there was space, water, and asphalt.

When the boy's grandfather died, they had tried to arrange for Uncle Aliyan to attend the funeral. He needed a pass since he lived in Jordan, so they asked the mukhtar to put in a request with the military governor. After a long wait, the military governor gave them a minute to present their case. Then he shook his head and left—no pass was issued. The grandfather was buried in a graveyard by the city wall. Aliyan stayed in Jordan until the emergence of the Palestinian Authority twenty years later. He returned to his homeland just once on a tourist visa that was easy to get. Sitting on his father's grave, he wept as he had never wept before.

"Men don't weep," they told him.

"Those with any feelings do," he replied.

A few years later, Aliyan died in Amman, and so did his tears.

"But I really want to be an astronaut," the boy repeated now, tears on his cheeks.

"As the saying goes, my boy, power corrupts," his father explained. "Power corrupts . . ."

At school, teacher Mahmoud al-Hallaq went missing.

The boy's heart pounded whenever class time approached, but the teacher never returned. People said that an army patrol had taken him prisoner, that someone had turned him in for writing *Free Palestine* on a building near Jabel Mukaber.

On Friday, the boy went to bed unusually early. He hugged his pillow, facing the wall. The cracks along the surface were close enough to breathe into. As he grew drowsier, the lines seemed to widen. In them he saw, or thought he saw, teacher Mahmoud asking him, in front of the class, *What do you want to be?* and him answering, *An astronaut*—making all the students laugh. There was his mother, rushing to rescue him from their mockery, while his father kept echoing: *Power corrupts. What do we have? No space, no water, no air. It's all occupied.*

The cracks opened up and turned into stars. An insect emerged and became a spaceship bound in chains. The boy grabbed the heavy chains and entered the wall. He saw an entire galaxy plated in blue lead. A solitary six-pointed star seemed to be at the center of everything. His father's friend once said that the six-pointed star was Canaanite. The one before him now was inimical, devouring all the other stars, turning the entire sky into lead, entangling everything—humans, Umm Hamdan's chickens, the Khan al-Zeit Market, the Lion's Gate, the Makassed Hospital where his younger brother would go to be treated for a chronic breathing problem. He saw protesters yelling in the galaxy: *Revolution till victory!* The leftist Abu Aysar shouted: *Revolutionaries don't die!* And yet lead is very heavy, and the science teacher Mahmoud was in jail. People said he'd studied chemistry at the University of Jordan; some wondered if he'd made materials for protesters. Were there teachers who could show the boy how to operate a spaceship?

The boy bumped his head against the wall and woke to a new morning. He'd been trying to fill the spaceship with hot fuel so it could take off, and now felt warm liquid against his leg. Screams suddenly resounded within the house. His father was silent, and the women were all gathered. His younger brother had died. Their shared bed was soaked with his private fuel. The spaceship did not take off.

"It happened at night," his father said. "He was sleeping beside you . . . We found him asphyxiated. It looks as though he swallowed his tongue."

They went to the cemetery at noon, by the Lion's Gate. They prayed in the al-Aqsa Mosque, then buried the body and returned home.

"Where's my brother going now?" he asked his father.

"Inshallah, to heaven," his father said.

"Okay, but where's heaven?"

"In the sky."

"You mean he's going to be an astronaut?"

"No, son, he'll be a sky flyer, one of the birds of paradise."

"I want to be a bird of paradise too. I want to be a sky flyer."

His grieving father rubbed his hands together in despair. "Go and tell that to the military governor."

"I will." The boy rushed away.

His father figured he was hiding somewhere. But then an hour passed with no sign of him. He went looking for the boy and started worrying. People returning to Jabel Mukaber near the station called his name. No one found him.

Hours later, a police patrol brought the boy back. He had stood in front of the control post and asked to see the military governor. He told them he wanted to be an astronaut. The police leveled accusations against the father, stating that it was wrong to incite children to commit crimes. Children had to understand reality and construct dreams that made sense. They handed the boy over to his family.

Years later, after numerous conflicts, more roads were closed and more barriers were erected by the city entrance. They turned into permanent checkpoints. The boy's planets, stars, and galaxies gradually disappeared. The six-pointed star consumed even more of the cosmos.

The small room was now the boy's alone. He brought colored chalk home from school—blue, red, and green—and drew galaxies and constellations on the wall and a spaceship taking off without fuel. The wall was collapsing because it had been poorly built and no new permits for construction were available in the city. A new settlement sprang up nearby, and the man in charge offered his father an opportunity to purchase a house. He refused, despite their pressure. The household consisted of a father, mother, and boy who wished to be an astronaut.

After high school, the boy studied at al-Quds University in the town of Abu Dis, near the eight-meter wall that separated it from Jerusalem. The university also had a modest branch inside the city. His father died, and the dilapidated house was passed down to him and his mother.

Representatives of the Israeli settlement projects called him in. They bargained with him, threatened him. On the table they placed a large check, along with a file that outlined the details of his life. They would make him an astronaut, a doctor in physics, a traverser of galaxies, anything, provided that he gave up the house. *Well, boy, what do you want to be when you grow up?* he remembered his old teacher asking.

With shaky hands, he ripped up the file and tore the check in two.

"I want my own house!" he declared to the enemy. "I don't want galaxies. I just want to be myself. A pox on space and physics!"

DIARY OF A JERUSALEM TEACHER

BY RAFIQA OTHMAN

Al-Sa'diyya

Translated by Roger Allen

T hat morning, silence veiled the city. I went up the steps by the Damascus Gate, heading from al-Sa'diyya in East Jerusalem to my job in West Jerusalem. The quarters of the city were slowly waking up. Peasant women started arriving from their villages with baskets on their heads. Each wanted to grab a strategic spot on the Damascus Gate steps or in niches of the towering wall. They would try to sell early, before the city patrols arrived, argued with them, and confiscated their goods—fruits and vegetables and homemade items, mostly. Every day they put up with all the hardship and inconvenience. They would set out at dawn with the early morning call to prayer, and go through the wall separating Bethlehem from Jerusalem, following the "cultural tracks" to avoid confrontations. Every woman knew her particular corner under the shade of the Old City wall.

A newspaper salesman, Amm Mahfouz, sat by the gate entrance. He was sorting the newspapers and dailies for passersby. "Get the latest news!" he shouted. "Jerusalem's calling you! Digs . . . settlements . . . house demolitions . . . raids on al-Aqsa . . . al-Aqsa uprising . . . arrests . . .

property and house sequestration . . . land confiscation
. . . changing procedures . . . All for three shekels! That's
the way it is, folks!"

I was curious, so I purchased that day's *al-Quds* newspaper; it could at least keep me amused on the bus. I starting hurrying to the stop.

On my way, I ran across a vendor of arak sous. He had
a red tarboosh on his head and matching trousers, like the
ones worn by clowns. He was pulling his cart, decorated
with finery and colored roses befitting a bride's bouquet.
The vendor took his usual niche, near Amm Mahfouz.
With a tiny bit of mace between his thumb and index finger, he hailed passersby and invited them to try his drink.
His presence seemed picturesque, like one of Jerusalem's
columns, an authentic Arab tradition of long standing.
People were drawn by the sheer artistry with which he
poured cold arak and almond juice for them.

As I reached the top of the steps at the Damascus Gate,
I was out of breath. Close by, a large group of city workers,
both young and old, were gathered with their tools. Their
clothes revealed their particular trades; one man was practi-
cally dressed in white paint splatters. All hoped that a Jewish
contractor would pass by and choose them by virtue of their
apparent strength or youth. Whenever a contractor drove
up, they would stare and start shoving each other. God,
what a sad sight! Jerusalem folk fighting each other every
day just to afford a bite . . . It leaves a lump in your throat.

Then, a lovely voice drifted through the air: "O
splendid home, O flower of the cities." Fairuz! Her song
was coming from one of the stores:

*O Jerusalem, O Jerusalem, O Jerusalem, O city of
the prayer
Our eyes are set out to you every day
They walk through the porticos of the temples
Embrace of the old churches
And take the sadness away from the mosques*

I felt an inner tranquility as the song ended: "By our hands the peace will return to Jerusalem." How true was the person who called her voice angelic! If only you knew, Fairuz! The people of Jerusalem have never experienced solidarity like yours and Hany Shaker's, when he sang "At the Door of Jerusalem": "Every city sleeps with its deep dreams, but not the eyes of Jerusalem . . . Eyes tell us Jerusalem will stay, it will not die."

Walking along, I picked up a wonderful aroma—Arab bread and Jerusalem cake decorated with sesame! No doubt, it wafted out of Amm Hasan's place in Musrara. It penetrated the cells in my nose and kindled all my senses. I so longed to buy one of those sesame cakes. But I didn't have time now; I had a bus to catch.

I waited for it on Sultan Suleiman Street, opposite Zedekiah's Cave, a true archeological marvel. Our history teacher described it as the biggest cave to stretch beneath the city. The entrance was under the Old City wall. During the reign of Sultan Suleiman, it was called the Cotton Cave because cotton and linen were stored there.

How many riddles and secrets are concealed in the Old City—stories and myths buried behind every single pillar. As Palestinian poet Tamim al-Barghouti writes, "In Jerusalem, the stones of the buildings are quoted from the Bible and the Quran." And once you have been to Jerusalem, "you will only see her, wherever you look."

How beautiful you are, City of Peace, pasture of heavenly faiths. Everything in you pulsates with life. In you, history is recorded in heroic deeds. Your buildings, your alleys, your quarters—they all bear the fragrance of history. Behind every stone a piece of history is recorded, or an amazing legend. How high are your walls, and how stubborn. If only I were a good poet so I could sing your praises, like my colleague, the poet Doctor Mo'tazz, the Jerusalem celebrity who composed an ode about his love for Iliyya al-Bahiyya in his final poetry collection, *A Letter to My Lady:*

> *Jerusalem is still the most beautiful in our world*
> *Like a pearl clothed in diamonds and gold.*
> *I am Qays, and the land of Jerusalem is my Layla;*
> *On the morrow, I long to be her lover . . .*

When I and others heard that poem, tears filled our eyes. He delivered it in a loud voice in the Hakawati Theater. His words pierced the ears and reached the heart. I will never forget that moment, especially after Israeli soldiers broke into the theater. "You have five minutes to leave the building!" one soldier barked. His broken Arabic ended everything.

When my bus arrived, I sat in the back, watching people getting on and off as we headed to the central station. I did this every day. But this particular morning felt strangely different. I was anxious. I leafed through *al-Quds*, looking for my horoscope in the hope that it might calm my nerves. But it didn't: "Today will be inauspicious for people under this sign. Use both wisdom and caution in making personal decisions."

I pricked up my ears and listened to the morning news on the radio. It announced, in Hebrew, that the authorities were going to close the city's streets and entrances at noontime for Jerusalem Day celebrations, the Israeli holiday commemorating the "reunification" of the city.

I muttered the two verses of refuge from the Quran, and pleaded to God. *God, protect us from what's to come!* I told myself.

Before I could finish my prayers, the bus driver stopped by the separation line. Several passengers asked what was going on, and he explained that a suspicious package had been found in the transfer station. The armed forces were going to blow it up. We had to stay put and listen to instructions until the danger had passed.

Meanwhile, my nerves were screaming. My watch's hands were moving so slow I thought they had stopped, along with my heart and mind. I checked the time when the bus was supposed to leave, my gaze focused on the Museum on the Seam sitting on the line that separated East and West Jerusalem. Its face still showed the scars from 1967. I remembered my father talking about the powerful forces on the other side of that spot.

An explosion interrupted my thoughts—they'd blown up the suspicious package. I started counting the seconds before the bus left. I had another worry: I was bound to be late for work, and Director Roni would confront me about it.

The bus stopped on Jaffa Street and let in a short, fat, brown-skinned police officer with a gun strapped to her waist. She started looking at passengers' faces as though searching for prey. She went over to an Arab who looked over sixty. He was carrying a black plastic bag and smoking a cigarette, not bothering anyone. Without hesitation, the officer stopped alongside him and demanded his identity card. The man took out a pile of papers and started riffling through them. Eventually, he found his ID and handed it over.

"Where are you going?" the cop asked in broken Arabic. "What's in the bag? What's your workplace called? What's the address? Is this you in the photograph?"

Worry struck the man's face. His hands shook, and the plastic bag dropped. Now everyone could see the contents: four falafel patties, sesame cake, boiled eggs. The poor man was embarrassed. He got up and clumsily collected the rolling patties, then sat down again. The officer looked at him and the photo on his blue ID, comparing. She told him to leave the bus with her, and they both stepped off. I stared through the window to see what would happen, but they disappeared from view.

Eventually, I reached the school on Avraham Stern Street in West Jerusalem, panting as though I had just run the city's annual marathon. There was the school director, lying in wait and stopping latecomers—students and teachers alike.

"Why so late?" Roni asked.

"Bad h-horoscope," I stuttered, "then a s-suspicious package. The bus—"

"Go," he interrupted, "and don't be late again!"

I went into the class for deaf children. They were performing a play. Some were carrying friends on their shoulders and reciting "God is great" as separate words. It looked as though they were in a parade or demonstration, carrying Palestinian flags that they'd made themselves. I figured they were acting out a typical Palestinian street.

They moved around the classroom without following the daily routine. Some of them made violent gestures, using signs I'd never encountered. Anger seemed to seep from their hearts. I tried calming them down and getting them to do other activities, but I failed. I needed to think of a way to help them relieve their revolutionary sentiments without losing sight of the fact that they were Palestinian children in a school with both Arab and Jewish students.

I grabbed some coloring books and handed them out. The deaf students started scribbling, and now there was a pervasive silence. God be praised! It appeared these books could pacify them.

As I wandered around the students, I saw that they were fixated on the uprising. One of them had drawn children throwing stones at soldiers; a girl was sketching a Palestinian flag atop the Dome of the Rock; a boy depicted a child standing in front of an Israeli tank. Here was the funeral for a martyr who was being carried on people's shoulders. There was a popular demonstration with Palestinian flags raised in the air. Amid glaring colors, the flag was all over these pages—some even featured a map of Palestine.

My heart thumped at the thought of Roni suddenly appearing and seeing the pictures. *They'll fire me,* I told myself, *accusing me of incitement. Good God, what am I supposed to do? Palestinian flags in a Jewish school, not to mention maps of Palestine.*

I had a number of concerns. On the one hand, it was my duty to respect my students' affiliations; on the other, I had to adhere to a profession that was now subject to non-Arab supervisors. I started glancing at the classroom door, like someone keeping a flock safe from ravenous wolves, in case someone came in and saw the drawings. Eventually, a non-Arab teacher did enter, and of course spotted some of the art. I did my best to keep her occupied so she wouldn't see the rest. She seemed angry but didn't say a word. When she left, it was as though she had not seen anything. Nevertheless, I couldn't stop the feeling that my career was in crisis. I could just imagine how Roni might react to this scene: *Get out of here. Shalom!*

Two days before, one of my students had ripped up the Israeli flag, and Roni came to the classroom to punish her. The girl huddled against me in fear. Hatred filled Roni's eyes, but he didn't utter a single word. He gave the girl a cruel look, his hands shaking, but then left without explaining himself.

Now, the school bell interrupted my thoughts. I quickly collected the suspect coloring books and hid them in my briefcase, which I then stored in the classroom locker. I told the students that I was going to analyze their drawings for my research because they were so important—too important to hang on the walls like usual.

When I left that afternoon, I brought the briefcase. I felt as though I were carrying a suspicious package or time bomb. That was especially the case as I entered the central station, the site of many of my nightmares. I felt compelled to clutch it against my chest. When my turn came to be inspected, I was terrified. The guard took the briefcase from me.

"What's inside?" he asked.

"Personal papers," I said.

My face turned red; an intense heat seared my body. My hands were trembling. This was the first time I had been subjected to this kind of questioning. The guard opened the briefcase without asking me. He started sifting through the pictures and took a seat. With each page, he shook his head.

A long line of travelers waited behind. Some complained about the delay, others looked on curiously and tried to get a glimpse of the pictures. All of it upset me.

The guard asked for my identity card and at the same time picked up his phone. He made me stand to one side, kept my ID and briefcase, and placed the pictures on the floor beside his tiny, overcrowded desk. All eyes were focused on me. Comments in various languages reached my ears. I could hardly stand, and almost fainted under the glare of the boiling sun, but kept staring over at the pictures. I just waited there until the guard forgot about me.

A tall female police officer with blond hair eventually

arrived with a gun on her hip and handcuffs. She spoke with the guard and gave me looks that were hardly comforting. She told me to pick up my briefcase and led me into a small room for interrogation. Then she went back to collect the pictures.

But I was calm, no longer concerned with consequences. Right before the female officer had arrived, and totally by chance, a street sweeper had come by, assumed the papers were trash, and put them in his wastebasket. He then disappeared, without sensing what was going on.

After half an hour, the blond police officer returned to the interrogation room. Red in the face, she was clearly frustrated. She started my interrogation all over again and used a nasty, threatening tone of voice. Her Hebrew had a noticeable English accent.

"Where are those subversive pictures?" she asked. "Take them out. Why have you hidden them? I'm not letting you leave till you hand them over."

"Believe me," I replied, "I don't have any papers in my briefcase. I don't know what you're talking about. Search me if you wish."

The officer took my case, opened it, and searched every possible crevice. She turned it upside down and emptied the contents: personal items. She spread them out on the table in front of her and looked at them, then at me. I stood with my head held high; I was no longer scared. The officer now took me into a tiny, airless inspection room, and checked my body from head to toe.

"Okay," she said, "put your things back in the case and wait here. Don't leave."

"Fine."

I stayed in that stifling room, sweat pouring off me. As I sat there at the table, I reviewed everything that had happened in my mind, despite a terrible headache. *I really need some rest.* I recited the two verses of refuge again and asked God to rescue me from this situation. My mother was probably wondering why I was late, worried; I pictured the family preparing food, setting up the table, waiting for me.

After a full hour, the police officer came back and asked me to sign a register: "If the pictures reappear, you will be summoned." Her words were tinged with malice.

I signed as requested.

"You can leave now. I'm releasing you."

I set off as fast as possible. Two contrasting emotions played in my heart: happiness at escaping and sorrow about losing the pictures. I caught the bus to East Jerusalem and slumped in my seat, totally wrecked. My head spun uncontrollably, replaying the incident at the station. What if I had called to the sweeper to leave the pictures?

I have no idea whether it was God-inspired wisdom or fear of prison that had made me stay silent in order to escape . . . Yes, it had to be the same wisdom my horoscope had mentioned that morning. Praise be to God— my students and I had avoided inhumane treatment.

Finally, the bus reached the Jaffa Gate, alongside the Tower of David. I stepped off and walked toward Herod's Gate, following the sounds of chaos. Barriers had been erected at the ends of streets, which teemed with armed soldiers keeping guard on Palestinians.

Settlers, men and women, were dancing in circles, leaping into the air, hugging each other, carrying Israeli flags. They chanted anti-Palestinian slogans in Hebrew and recited phrases from the Torah. One slogan was being repeated over and over again, burning my ears: *"Yerushalayim shel zahav"*—"Jerusalem of gold." Some Jerusalemites stood in rows on the side of the street behind the soldiers; they were yelling their opposition to the unification of Jerusalem: "Jerusalem's Arab, neither East nor West! No to unification! Jerusalem's ours, Jerusalem's ours!"

I stood in the crowd watching the scene. How I wished to go up in a balloon and fly over the city—its houses, its alleys, and its walls—so I could draw my own picture of this fearful, sad land.

One month before the end of the school year, Director Roni summoned me to a disciplinary hearing. It was based on a flimsy pretext: nonadherence to daily attendance. They dispensed with my services at the school

THE SUN STILL SHINES

BY DIMA AL-SAMMAN

Musrara

Translated by Max Weiss

The dawn call to prayer rang out from the holy al-Aqsa Mosque. It spread out over the breadth of Jerusalem and its surrounding villages, climbed the peaks of its mountains, cascaded down its plains, plunged into the depths of its wadis . . . The call liberated the enslaved through the reverence of the pious and the humility of those penitent supplicants seeking to draw closer to God.

There rose the sounds of the city folk starting to stir, their eyelids still sealed, sleep numbing their bodies. Recitations of the shahada, the glorification of God's name, and prayer: words that emanated from the caverns of their chests, slow and languorous, lounging as if on a tongue chair in the hollow of their mouths, emerging taut yet somehow suffused in lackadaisical ease: *I bear witness that there is no god but God . . . and I bear witness that Muhammad is the messenger of God. We are all God's dominion and so am I . . .*

"Abu Omar . . . Abu Omar!" Salma crowed as she tried to awaken her husband, Fares. "Wake up . . . It's the dawn call to prayer, you're going to miss the congregational prayer at al-Aqsa."

"I bear witness that there is no god but God," Fares yammered as he got up. "I bear witness that Muhammad is the messenger of God. Go on ahead of me and do your ablutions, Umm Omar. I'll be right behind you."

Salma went to carry out her ablutions and came back praising God. Her voice cracked with surprise when she heard her husband's snoring as he lay there still, deep in sleep. She nudged him.

"My love . . . you're going to be late for prayer. Why are you such a sleepyhead? Through the window I can hear men from the neighborhood exclaiming God's praise. They're going to notice your absence and start asking about you. Inshallah, everything's all right, you look tired. Where's your usual energy? Tell me, what's the matter, Fares?"

He struggled to open his eyes, then sluggishly rolled out of bed, muttering, "There is no strength except in God," as he tried to comfort his wife. "Nothing, Umm Omar . . . nothing at all . . . It just feels like I didn't get enough sleep. I've been feeling on edge, which makes it hard for me to get any rest."

"What's wrong? Anything I should be nervous about too?"

"No, don't worry . . . don't worry, Salma."

Fares performed his ablutions, threw on the white dishdasha he always wore to prayer, and hurried toward the door, repeating, "There is no strength except in God," and mumbling words that splintered apart on his tongue, and which Salma couldn't easily make out.

"What are you saying? I can't hear you . . . Are you speaking to me?"

"No, no," he replied, a little agitated. "I was just praying, Umm Omar . . . Praying to God on your behalf."

"All right, goodbye then, go with God."

Fares shut the door behind him, leaving Salma confused about what was up with him. She knew her husband well. He would never hide anything from her. There must be something that was bothering him. *What could he be hiding?* she wondered. She had grown accustomed to being included in all of his affairs, no matter how incidental. She was his refuge and his home, his partner, his friend, and his lover, which is how he always described her to strangers and intimate friends alike. Their marriage had lasted more than thirty-five years. They had tasted life's sweetness and bitterness, relying on one another at every obstacle they faced, overcoming them together. They would never let a simple matter get in the way of their beautiful life together. They had a special relationship, a model for a successful marriage and blissful family life, which they demonstrated everywhere, on any occasion.

They had fallen in love as adolescents, and their feelings had only grown over the years. They got married despite Salma's family's opposition. Her family was well off. Salma's father owned a contracting firm and bought and sold properties worth millions of dollars. Fares's father, by contrast, owned a wooden cart. Every morning, he would visit a beloved bakery in the Musrara neighborhood, near the historic Damascus Gate, where he filled up his cart with Jerusalem sesame bread, carefully placing it on his head and carrying it to his regular spot on the sidewalk across from Schmidt's Girls College, shouting out a familiar melody to passersby: "Hot sesame bread! Falafel, fried eggs, HOT sesame bread . . . Step right up, get over here, come and get the good stuff . . . HOT sesame bread!"

The schoolgirls squawked orders at him, asking for a piece of bread and a mouthwatering ball of falafel, some also requesting a fried egg with crushed green za'atar wrapped in newspaper. Afterward, he would cheerfully set off for school, clutching his daily take, counting the money during his break between classes.

Memory transported Salma back to her time at the Terra Santa School inside Jerusalem's Old City walls. She had lived in a villa located in a posh neighborhood of the village of Beit Hanina. Most mornings her father would give her a ride in his glitzy Mercedes, dropping her right in front of the New Gate, where the school was located. On some days she took the bus, when her father couldn't get up in time. A lot of his work meetings happened at night and could last until very late.

On those mornings, she would arrange to meet her friend Leila, who lived nearby, at the bus stop at seven on the dot. The two of them went together.

It was a thrill to ride with her friend all the way to the last stop at the Damascus Gate. There, they continued on foot for about half a kilometer to the school. They would often bump into their schoolmates at the hill just outside the New Gate, and then they would all walk as a group, recalling funny incidents in class, giddy with laughter the whole way, attracting the attention of everyone they passed. Neither Salma nor Leila would miss an opportunity to buy sesame bread from Uncle Abu Fares's famous cart.

One morning, Salma and Leila were nearing Abu Fares's stand when they were surprised to see that the vendor wasn't there but instead a handsome young man. He was showing customers the utmost respect. As Salma gazed upon him, she remembered who he was . . . It was Fares . . . Yes, that was his name. She would never forget what had happened in August, about two months before, on the steps outside the Damascus Gate when she happened to slip on a banana peel, lose her footing, and fall splat on her back, spilling everything she had been carrying in her backpack: paper and other supplies she had bought for the coming school year. A handsome, well-dressed young man, who came across as both mild mannered and well bred, rushed over and helped her to her feet. He gathered up her things, returned them to the bag, and then handed her some tissues so she could clean off her dirty clothes. He didn't walk away until he could make sure she was all right, offering to accompany her to a clinic nearby. Salma thanked him in embarrassment, insisting that she was fine. She hurried to get lost amid the crowds of people, wishing the earth would swallow her whole.

It was a Saturday, the day of the week when the Old City burst with citizens and tourists and visitors from the northern part of the country that had been occupied in 1948. Settlers spread out far and wide, especially religious ones who would cut their way to the Buraq Wall, which they call the Wailing Wall.

Salma made it to her friend Mona's house in the tense Christian Quarter, her feelings a mix of anger at whoever had dropped the banana peel that had gotten her into this mess and the kind of humiliation that would afflict any young lady who fell down in plain sight of so many others. In spite of all that, she was intoxicated by a strange mood she had never experienced before. It felt as though her heart were dancing for joy.

Salma wouldn't have known who that kindhearted, handsome man was if she hadn't heard another young man at the top of the stairs call out to him: "Come on, Fares, we're late!"

The impression she got of this Fares would not leave her mind, resting just beneath her eyelids all night. She longed to run into him again, hoping fate was on her side.

Now here she was today, seeing him once more. Her heart nearly flew out of her rib cage, pumping blood into her cheeks and telegraphing her feelings to the world. Fares was busy selling to his customers as she stood there, nailed to the ground, staring at him, bewildered. What could he be doing behind the cart? What was his relationship to the owner? When Leila noticed her confusion, she nudged Salma and asked what was wrong. Then, Fares met Salma's eyes. Blood flushed his face, as if revealing a secret he had tried to hide, outing him.

The customers' voices surged louder, everyone jostling to pay for their sesame bread and be on their way. Fares took stock of the situation, and when Salma's turn came he wrapped her bread in a plastic bag and refused to take any money . . . but she insisted on paying. It all happened in plain view of Leila, who was swiveling back and forth between their faces, unsure how to make sense of what was happening.

Leila grabbed her friend's hand and gave it a squeeze, encouraging her to start walking, then asked, "What's up?" Salma explained that this young man was *the* Fares she had told her about, from the day she went to visit Mona in the Christian Quarter.

"Oh my God," Leila said, laughing. "Where's your brain? The son of a *street vendor*, my dear? Don't tell me you have a crush on a sesame bread seller. He probably dropped out of school and is filling in for his father. Remember who you are, girl. Don't let your emotions drag you into something that's going to be unacceptable to your family."

Salma didn't respond. She was in a state of shock. *Does Fares go to school?* she wondered. *Does he now work the cart with his father?* Questions crammed into her head, making her feel like it might explode.

She was depressed by the time she made it home, shutting herself in her room and refusing to have lunch with her family. Her mother tried to cajole her into saying why she wasn't feeling well, but Salma lied that she hadn't been able to finish all the problems in her math exam and wasn't sure she had done well enough to pass.

Her mother held her close to her chest, promising to talk to the teacher and convince them to give her some private tutoring in order to improve her performance.

That evening, Salma's family gathered to watch television and talk. At exactly eight p.m., when the Jordanian news broadcast came on which her father watched religiously to follow global political developments, Salma got up to go to her room. She didn't have much interest in politics.

The news digest began:

The Arab League recognizes the Palestine Liberation Organization as the "sole and legitimate representative of the Palestinian people" and accepts it as a full member of the league.

At dawn this morning, dozens of Israeli occupation soldiers stormed the house of the sesame bread seller Omar al-Farran, also known as Abu Fares, who lives in the Bab Hutta neighborhood of the Old City of Jerusalem. He was taken to the Maskobiyeh Detention Center for questioning regarding the bombing that took place about two weeks ago on Jaffa Street in West Jerusalem, in which two people were killed and scores were injured.

Salma sat back down. Her mother looked at her, until Salma explained herself.

"What a shame . . . That's the vendor we buy sesame bread from every morning, Mom."

The broadcast included a special report on the family

of Uncle Abu Fares. Salma learned that he was the son of a martyr and had grown up without a father since the age of seven. His mother cleaned houses to support him and his sister who was two years his junior. He had a daughter who was married and lived in Amman, as well as three sons: Fares, sixteen; Saed, fourteen; and Raed, twelve. All of them were enrolled at the Islamic Orphans' School in Jerusalem. His wife, Umm Fares, worked as a seamstress out of their house in Bab Hutta.

Salma fled to her room. She couldn't hold back tears. Shutting her eyes tight, she drifted back to the moment when Fares met her gaze. He was unmistakably happy about meeting her, but sorrow had also peered from his eyes. She cried long and hard that evening.

Yaaaaa . . . Love leaves us paralyzed in the face of our helplessness. We aren't capable of running away but aren't capable of moving ahead either. Having feelings for you could be a mistake, Fares. But who ever said I want to be right? It feels so good to feel you with my mind, to see you with my heart, to love you with all of my soul.

Salma wanted to get in touch with him, to ease his burden, but how?

She didn't sleep that night and the next morning she didn't go to school. She was extremely fatigued. Her mother asked the doctor to make a house call. The doctor assured her that Salma was suffering from nothing more serious than exhaustion and anxiety, possibly from the stress of midterm exams.

The phone rang, slicing through Salma's reverie. She

wondered who could be calling so early in the morning. Perhaps it was good news . . . She lifted the telephone to her ear to discover that it was her daughter, Amal.

"Good morning, Mother."

She noticed a quiver in her daughter's voice.

"What's wrong, Amal? Everything all right, inshallah?"

"Mom, didn't Dad tell you yet?"

"Tell me what?"

"Soldiers opened fire at Basel yesterday afternoon." Amal exploded in tears. "He was coming out of school in a peaceful march down Nablus Street and they detained him. Mom, it's the first night Basel has ever slept away from home . . . I have no idea how he's doing, whether he's injured or what."

Salma was shocked. She now understood what her husband had been trying to keep from her, knowing how much she already worried about her oldest grandchild, Basel. Maybe he wanted to break the news gently so that she would be less distraught.

Salma suppressed a wail as tears leaked from her eyes. "Do you know the families of any of his friends who might have been with him?" She tried to remain calm so as not to add to Amal's anxiety. "Have you been in touch with any of them?"

"Yes, we learned from his friend Fuad, our neighbor's son, that Basel was shot in the leg and collapsed to the ground before a battalion of soldiers jumped on him and beat the hell out of him, Mom. Then they dragged him over to their military jeep and threw him inside."

"Dear God. Where is he now? I mean, which hospital?"

"I heard he's at Hadassah Ein Kerem."

"What a bunch of criminals. How can they detain a child? He isn't even thirteen."

"They arrested him along with kids who are even younger, Mom. They have no conscience, there's no mercy in their hearts."

"There is no strength except in God. Don't worry, I'm sure they'll release him. He doesn't have a record. He'll be back with you soon, Amal, don't worry."

"My God . . . But where's Dad? Is he back from dawn prayer yet? His cell phone's off."

"No, he's not back yet."

Just then Fares opened the front door and walked inside.

"Wait, hold on a sec, Amal, your father's just arrived."

Fares came in heavy footed as Salma handed him the phone.

"It's Amal. Why didn't you tell me, Fares?" she reproached.

"I was going to tell you today for sure, but I didn't want you to lose any sleep over it. I had a rough night, didn't sleep a wink."

Fares tried to comfort his daughter. He was a skilled lawyer who specialized in administrative detention. "Don't worry, my dear, your son will come home soon. Trust in God. I'll make all the necessary phone calls and go see him in the hospital tomorrow. Everything's going to be fine, inshallah."

Fares hung up and got into bed, asking for quiet so he

could fall back asleep, if only for an hour. He had a difficult day ahead of him.

Salma couldn't sleep. Memories assaulted her, dragging her once again to her adolescence. She talked to herself: *My God! What's the matter with this family? I wonder
. . . is the struggle passed down from generation to generation?* She remembered Uncle Abu Fares, son of the martyr whose soul left his body in 1948 as he stood on the
Old City walls, holding a rifle. For his involvement in
the bombing on Jaffa Street, he was sentenced to life in
prison, although his soul rose to the heavens as a martyr
after seven years. He had been unwell and couldn't get
medical attention.

His father's death shook young Fares to the core. He had
been determined to distinguish himself academically so
that he could achieve his dream, one born from his father's arrest: becoming a famous lawyer, standing before
the justices at the high court, fighting the ruling against
his father, defending him to the hilt, calling and questioning witnesses. After a careful deliberation the judge
would pronounce a verdict of innocence and his father
would be brought out, carried aloft on people's shoulders,
everyone chanting the name of the liberated, all of them
praising the brilliance of his son Fares. Fares would enjoy a bliss he had never felt before. His family would
take pride in him, bringing back a smile to his mother's
lips after she had suffered so terribly in her husband's
absence.

But his dream never came true. He entered law

practice after graduating from Ain Shams University in Egypt—and not even two years later, death ripped away the head of the household.

Fares had been one of the smartest and most determined students in his law school cohort. He didn't want to squander the competitive scholarship he'd received from a Jerusalemite foundation: to continue getting the full tuition amount, his grade point could not fall below a B average. So he worked hard to maintain an A throughout his academic career. He returned home after four years—four years of missing Jerusalem, his family, and Salma, who stayed in touch via handwritten letters. They had become closer prior to university, thanks to cultural competitions that brought together schools from all over Jerusalem, allowing them to explore how much they liked each other despite their very different milieus. Fares stayed abreast of all her news, nervous that her father would force her to marry her cousin Atef, a doctor ten years her senior who worked at Hadassah Hospital Mount Scopus. Atef was an excellent surgeon. After completing his education at Damascus University, he had received an academic scholarship at the Sorbonne, where he specialized in brain surgery. Because of the rarity of that specialization, Hadassah offered him an attractive salary to head their division.

Atef had asked Salma to marry him a few years before, but she refused under the pretense of wanting to complete her degree and then find a job so that she could get some real-world experience before burying herself in the responsibilities of caring for a husband and children. She graduated from Birzeit University with a degree in English literature and became a high school teacher.

Fares trained to practice law under the well-known counselor Abdel Fattah, who had been lawyering for more than forty-five years, during which time he hadn't lost a single case. He had always been distinguished for his cunning and intelligence, an extreme perspicacity that bored through anyone he questioned. When he became aware of Fares's brilliance, he took him under his wing as his right-hand man. In more than one setting, Counselor Abdel Fattah was able to discern just how honorable and trustworthy Fares was, sometimes by chance, other times through loyalty tests. As a result, he came to care deeply for him. As Fares grew more impressive in his eyes, he decided to offer him a full-time position in his office once he had completed his probationary period, providing him with a good salary that would ensure a comfortable life.

Counselor Abdel Fattah relied on Fares for a number of complex cases, and he never let him down. In fact, opposing counsel would try to avoid Fares as much as possible.

One afternoon, Fares came back from court in a cheerful mood after successfully arguing a case that had made his whole team nervous, regaling Counselor Abdel Fattah with the good news that their client had been exonerated. They laughed as Fares described how red the opposing counsel became when the final witness was called, especially after Fares presented certified documents confirming the soundness of the testimony. Just then, the phone rang, and the secretary handed it to Fares.

Counselor Abdel Fattah immediately noticed how the call affected the young man's demeanor.

Fares anxiously put down the phone and asked if he could leave the office for a bit, claiming he needed rest after two nights of preparing this case. Counselor Abdel Fattah was unconvinced, and demanded to know what could have so seriously changed his mood. He knew him too well: Fares would refuse to leave the office early no matter how tired he was; he had enviable vigor. Fares reluctantly revealed that Salma had called—her father intended to marry her to her cousin Dr. Atef, and refused to even entertain the idea of Fares as her groom. Salma had been crying uncontrollably, begging him to intervene however he could.

Counselor Abdel Fattah chuckled. "You solve other people's problems, but you can't even figure out your own little life, Fares! You're a well-respected lawyer, everybody can vouch for you. What is it, cat got your tongue?"

"The problem is her father's traditional, inflexible way of thinking, Counselor. He wants her to marry a man from a respectable family with Jerusalem roots, just like all the other elite Jerusalemite families who mistreat their daughters. They'd prefer that they remain unmarried rather than be wed to young men from families that are not of the right social class, according to their own definitions and standards." Fares shook his head. "I can't imagine losing Salma. I've been in love with her for nine years . . . I'd go ask for her hand right now, tell him she's not going to be with anyone other than me, and—"

"Take it easy, man, what the hell is wrong with you? Do you want to lose her forever? Have you gone mad? Where's your brain?"

"There's no rational mind or logic when it comes to matters of the heart, Counselor."

"I'm warning you, Fares: you shouldn't reach out to him. Leave it to me. I'll sort it out. Her father's an old friend of mine, I have the keys that can open him up. Trust in God and his humble servant. You know how proud I am of you. Don't worry, I won't let you down."

Reminiscing, Grandma Salma nodded her head, smiling sorrowfully. *My God! A human being can be so weak in the face of their problems!*

The doorbell rang. Amal and her husband Samir were at the door. Amal rushed toward her mother and buried her head in her shoulder, sobbing as Samir stood motionless. Salma looked at him and saw the sadness of the whole world in his eyes.

"What's the matter, son? What is it? Don't you trust Uncle Fares?"

He flung himself on the sofa without a word.

"Don't you trust your uncle?" she asked again.

"Ahhh, woman, my uncle . . . I trust him more than I trust myself, but I'm nervous about Basel's condition too . . . He's been hurt."

"Where's Dad?" Amal asked.

Salma let out a sigh she seemed to have held in for a lifetime. "Your father didn't sleep at all last night. He just now got into bed for a little rest."

At that moment Fares entered the living room. Amal ran over and started to cry into his chest. Her father held her, greeted his son-in-law, and then said to all three of them, while keeping his gaze fixed on his beloved wife Salma, "There's no reason to worry, everyone. Everything's going to be fine, inshallah."

"I'll make some coffee," Salma said. She smiled, trying to hide the tremors in her cheeks. As she hurried toward the kitchen, she wiped away a fugitive tear that escaped her eye.

Fares got ready to go visit Basel. The hospital had refused to allow his parents or anyone from the family to visit or even speak with him on the phone, but Fares would secure permission as his attorney.

Basel's room was under extraordinary surveillance, as though he were a most-wanted terrorist. Fares shook his head disdainfully at the sight, and asked to speak with the child prisoner alone.

Basel was lying in bed, eyes closed, his right wrist handcuffed to the frame. His leg was wrapped in gauze, stained red. Fares regarded his young grandson who had been forced to grow up too soon. Sorrow clawed at his heart. Innocence suffused the boy's face, still dreaming about games and toys. He was often combative at school, which led his teacher to discipline him. He still yearned for his mother's breast, falling asleep on top of her every night.

Fares stroked his grandson's head gently, then kissed him on the cheek. Basel struggled to open his eyes. He hadn't expected to find his grandfather right there before him. Over the past twenty-four hours he had been beaten and tortured. He remained silent for a beat, then coughed despite how badly it hurt. He pawed his grandfather's hand. Here was his best friend, the keeper of his secrets. It was nice to have him nearby. Basel called out to him the way he always did: "Greetings to Fares the Brave!"

Fares laughed with glee at his grandson, who was concealing his pain and trying to act like everything was normal. "Greetings to the grandson of Fares the Brave," he replied. "You had us worried, my friend. What happened to you? Tell me everything."

Basel looked around. "Where's my mom and dad? Where's my brother and sister? Where's Grandma Salma? Why didn't they come with you?"

"I'm here as your attorney, Basel, not as your grandfather."

Basel smiled. "Thank God you studied law, Grandpa."

Fares laughed as he pulled his grandson tightly to his chest, sensing how anxious and afraid he was. "I'm here to help you," he said. "I don't want you to worry. All you have to do is remember what happened to you when you got out of school as precisely as you can, and then tell me all about it. Leave the rest to your grandfather, who's also your friend."

When the consultation came to an end, Fares requested a detailed medical report on Basel's condition, then paid a visit to the public prosecutor's office, where he was able to acquire an order releasing the young man on a bond of five thousand shekels until the arraignment could be scheduled. The conditions included house arrest: Basel's father would be legally liable and violation could result in jail time as well as a penalty of ten thousand shekels.

At first Basel was happy to be home. He enjoyed the love and tenderness his family showed him, and received first-rate health care from a family friend who visited every evening to dress his wounds and monitor his progress.

Fortunately, this detention took place toward the end of the school year. Basel's mother convinced the school to excuse him from final exams. He received passing grades in all of his subjects so he wouldn't have to sacrifice the academic year either; the school simply awarded him the same grades he had earned in the past.

Then it was summer break, the time for vacations, activities. The first month passed uneventfully; in the second month, Basel tried unsuccessfully to come to terms with being imprisoned at home. Each morning he would watch his siblings and his friends and the neighborhood children heading out to their summer camps and clubs. In the afternoons his friends would gather to play soccer at the field across from his home in Beit Hanina, while he was forbidden from setting foot beyond the doorstep or else his father would be subject to legal punishment.

He hated being home when others were in the house.

All his family members played the role of police officer, watching his movements and warning how dangerous it would be to go outside, especially given the electronic monitor locked around his ankle. It would emit a warning if he stepped out, or even if he made irregular movements while still inside.

One day, he and his brother Tareq were wrestling and sprinting around the house when the monitor's alarm suddenly went off. Within minutes, a phalanx of security agents came crashing in with a savagery that terrified his younger sister so much that she peed her pants. Nobody in the house knew what to do. The men asked if Basel had crossed the threshold.

This event bewildered Basel, and after they left he fell into a state of deep depression. He remained in his room and stopped interacting with the family.

Everyone was worried. Salma suggested throwing a big party for him on his thirteenth birthday, which was only two days away. It had been his wish the year before to have a party, but he ended up deciding against it because his sister Hoda was in the hospital getting her tonsils removed.

The entire family helped decorate the living room with balloons and colorful streamers, everyone except the birthday boy himself, who never left his bedroom.

All of Basel's schoolmates, friends, and neighbors were invited.

On the day of the party, the attendees trickled in, all bearing gifts. Music was playing. Everyone was drawn to the fancy table that had been set up off to the side of the living room, covered with delectable and mouthwatering sweets and snacks, as well as an assortment of soft drinks and juices. Despite all this, Basel wouldn't come out of his room. His mother tried to cajole him into making an appearance, begged him in tears, but it made no difference. His father failed too.

Salma suggested they send in Fuad, his best friend, but he came up short as well. Basel refused to even recognize his existence.

Fares went into Basel's room and sat beside him on the bed. "Basel, why won't you come out to celebrate your birthday? Don't you realize that everyone has come over to have fun with you? Do you want to embarrass the family? This behavior is irresponsible! Don't worry, I'm not going to beg, you can do whatever you want. I'm shocked, though. Are you truly the friend of Fares the Brave? You know I don't hang out with weaklings . . ."

Basel stayed silent.

"Well? Say something. Aren't you going to tell me why you won't come out?" He paused. "Fine, just cry all alone in here, then, we'll celebrate without you, we'll cut the cake without you. After the guests all leave, they'll make up their own stories about what's going on with you. I don't recognize you, Basel, so weak like this."

Fares was getting up when Basel lunged into his lap, crying. Fares held him while he wept. The little boy hadn't been able to cry since the raid on the house that had terrified everyone and kept the family from attending his cousin Ruba's wedding in Istanbul because they couldn't leave him home alone. Due to his house arrest, all were anxious to comfort him, to offer anything he asked for, to make up for the fact that he was stuck inside. Now they were throwing him a big birthday bash to lift his spirits—but he couldn't ignore their pitying looks. He detested those stares for reminding him of his fragility and powerlessness. Basel's innocent heart shot out his suppressed words like a volcano.

"My friend," Fares responded, "aren't you the one who told me that negative thoughts prevent a person from seeing the illuminated path, cause him to take the gloomy road that has no way out? This difficult time will pass, my friend, and all that will be left are the memories. Come back to life . . . don't retreat from it. If I retreated from life when my father was arrested, when the family home was demolished, or when Grandma Salma's father refused to let her marry me, I never would have succeeded, I never would have proven my worth . . . And I wouldn't have been up to the challenge anytime someone confronted me or tried to take something from me. Basel, I named your mother Amal, *hope*, because your grandmother and I overcame all those difficulties with hope and optimism."

"Sure, Grandpa, but things were different for you."

"They weren't different, my friend. You aren't the first person to be subjected to house arrest or to cause their family anxiety. It's not your fault. Don't be so hard on yourself." Fares squeezed his shoulder. "Everybody loves you, Basel. They've all come here to celebrate you. Come on, get up. Wash your face, put on your best clothes, splash on some cologne. Come say hello to your guests. I miss hearing you play the guitar. I miss your beautiful voice." He stood up to leave. "Don't take too long, otherwise we'll have to cut the cake without you. Ten minutes, no more."

Basel cast a look of gratitude toward his grandfather. A smile of relief curled across his lips.

The boy walked into the living room and the party. He played his guitar while everyone sang along to his grandfather's favorite song, "Make Your Dreams Come True":

> *Take care on those days when the world is hard on you*
> *Let your own hands make your dreams come true and*
> *just come a little closer*
> *If you can reach out and touch your dreams with your*
> *bare hands, you're sure to achieve them*
> *Don't insult anyone who supports your dreams, be*
> *sure to believe them*
> *Quit your worrying*
> *We only live once, there's no second chance*
> *Through the clouds I can see the sun poking through*
> *from far away*
> *Despite our concerns, we'll find hope once again . . .*

As the guests left, many raved that it was the best birthday party they had ever attended.

The next morning, Basel was notified that the trial would take place in two weeks. He received the news with his grandfather's favorite song ringing in his ears, just the way Fares the Brave had prepared him.

PART III

MOVING INTO DESPAIR

THIS IS JERUSALEM

BY MAJID ABU GHOSH
Kafr Aqab

Translated by Catherine Cobham

It was four in the morning when a dreadful pain woke me. My sister Aisha heard my groaning and rushed into the room. We lived together in the slums of Kafr Aqab.

"Salim, what's the matter with you?"

"I don't know," I said, winded. "I've got a really bad pain in my left side."

"I'll bring you some sedatives." She started to leave but then paused in the doorway. "In the morning, go see the doctor at the health center. Maybe there's something wrong with your kidneys."

"Hurry, please, my left side is about to explode!"

Some restless hours later, I walked to the health center in Kafr Aqab. All medical centers under the Israeli health insurance scheme had branches there. They'd even set up offices for the Ministry of Interior and the National Insurance Institute, both near the Qalandia checkpoint. We didn't have any reason to cross the checkpoint except to pray at al-Aqsa Mosque or the Church of the Holy Sepulchre.

Upon arriving, I showed my ID to an official so she could arrange an appointment. She examined it and then met my eyes.

"Mr. Salim, they've stopped your health insurance."

"Stopped it? Why?"

"They say here"—she looked at her computer screen—"that you must go to the Ministry of Interior to confirm your home address."

"You mean so I can replace the address that no longer exists in Sheikh Jarrah with the one here in Kafr Aqab?" I remembered our old home, near the center of Jerusalem, on the other side of the West Bank separation barrier.

"I don't know, but you have to check with the ministry. As things stand, we can only offer you emergency treatment."

"Thank you, madam."

We hadn't realized we'd left the crowded neighborhoods of Jerusalem and the Arnona property tax for worse crowding in Kafr Aqab, or that we'd voluntarily entered the Jerusalem "ghetto," behind the barrier.

In front of the Interior Ministry's office in Wadi Joz, I waited several hours until it was my turn to set up an appointment.

"Mr. Salim?" said the receptionist, a young woman.

"Yes, that's me."

"Your meeting with the department has been scheduled for six months from today."

"Six months?" My left side stung. "Why so long?"

"We have many people wanting appointments."

"But I need mine soon! I'm ill and need to see a doctor. My health insurance is suspended until I confirm my home address."

"Everybody who comes here has their own story."

I left Wadi Joz and walked by the Old City. In the presence of the so-called Wailing Wall, I desperately needed a cup of coffee. The pain in my left side was overwhelming, but far greater was the pain of oppression—the tyranny of occupation.

NOBLE SANCTUARY

BY MUHAMMAD SHURAIM

Al-Aqsa Mosque

Translated by Marilyn Booth

I t was already a few minutes past seven thirty a.m. when Hajja Aisha emerged from her sister's house, observing as she did the gray clouds and streaks of white amassing in the sky. The cold air stung her face and hands. She had been in this world for seventy-five years. Her sister was two years younger but could not accompany her; she had been permanently injured when a land mine went off while she was tending flock near the Green Line.

Walking as rapidly as she could through the side streets, Hajja Aisha was soon waiting for a taxi on the main road. The street was quiet, typical of a Friday morning, but cars passed from time to time. For nearly half an hour she stood waiting. She began to worry if she'd be able to reach the checkpoint between Bethlehem and Jerusalem early enough. *You really have to be there by nine thirty at the latest,* her sister had said, *if you hope to actually get into the al-Aqsa Mosque—that is, if they allow you in—before the Friday prayer starts at noon.* People routinely arrived at the checkpoint very early, because experience taught them that it would quickly become congested. And there were numerous procedures to get through, seemingly designed to keep people out, or at least to create serious delays.

Hajja Aisha's sister had heard this from people who had gone there intending to worship, and from workers who crossed to reach their work sites.

It's already too late for me to try getting there any other way, Hajja Aisha told herself. *All I can do now is to keep waiting for the taxi, and I'll tell the driver I'm ready to pay whatever to get to Bethlehem. Then from there, I'll have to figure something else out . . .*

Moments later, a lead-gray private car stopped in front of her. The driver was a dark-complexioned man in his fifties wearing a white robe and skullcap. Next to him sat a pale woman in a hijab, the wrinkles across her face suggesting she was around his age. The driver peered at Hajja Aisha.

"Going to the Noble Sanctuary, Hajja?" he asked.

"Yes, son. Take me to al-Aqsa, if you know a route that goes around the accursed crossing. I'm ready to pay whatever I need to."

"Why do you want to avoid the crossing? You're an elderly woman, you wouldn't—"

"They say it's closed."

"No, they reopened it this morning. Get in. Our compensation will be getting you there."

"God bless you! God make your day most fortunate! May all God's creatures learn to be like you."

Hajja Aisha opened the rear door, her right hand trembling. With her left hand she immediately gripped the handle fixed on the car ceiling, as though she feared the driver might change his mind and shoot off before she could settle into the backseat.

As the car moved, Hajja Aisha spoke: "So, then, that's where you're going, son? The sanctuary?"

"She is—my sister here, Umm Musaab. She's going to the sanctuary. Me, no. I can't! The occupation classified me with folks who are security risks, not allowed to enter Jerusalem at all. I'll take my sister as far as the checkpoint, and then I'll wait around in the Bethlehem markets until it's time for the Friday prayer. I'll attend it at the Mosque of Omar, and afterward wait for my sister at the checkpoint. I ask God's understanding, I ask God to give me the same credit I'd get praying at the holy al-Aqsa Mosque—I mean, I'll be getting as near to it as I can."

"God does right by us," Hajja Aisha said, "and blessed be all who care! Would it please God, or any of God's servants, to see what's become of the road to the Noble Sanctuary?"

Umm Musaab leaned sideways to look at Hajja Aisha in the rearview mirror. She said, "I think you must have been a bit late leaving home, Hajja. Especially since you were waiting for public transportation."

"It's my sister's house, dear. My home is in Amman. Believe me, it isn't like me to be late. I couldn't sleep, and neither could my sister, all night long. We were still awake when it was time to do our dawn prayers. We'd been listening to the radio, hoping to hear news about the crossing opening, after they closed it yesterday afternoon around prayer time. After praying, each of us leaned on our pillow and rested our head on our palm

Without realizing it, we must have both dozed off. And

I woke up just a bit ago and left the house as quickly as I could, hoping to get to Bethlehem, to find a driver who could take me to Jerusalem without having to go through the checkpoint, if I paid him what he wanted."

"Ah, I see now!" said the driver. "You can get into Jerusalem without going through the crossing since you have a tourist visa."

"No, son. I didn't come with a visa. I have a West Bank ID card, but I live with my son in Jordan."

"Why are you so set on getting to the sanctuary to-day," he asked, "when it would mean going through extra trouble and pain? You know the Aya, where the Quran said that God doesn't charge a soul with anything beyond its ability. When you learned that the crossing was closed, you should've just waited. Next Friday. Why the hurry? You're staying with your sister—"

Hajja Aisha sighed. "God alone knows what things will be like next Friday . . . I came over from Amman yesterday to visit my sister and so I could attend the Friday prayer at al-Aqsa, before my heart operation on Tuesday. They say it's a tough one."

"Oh, I'm so sorry, Hajja! If that's the way things are, then of course you've got a point. May God heal you and restore your health!"

Looking in the mirror, Umm Musaab said, "God keep you in good health, Hajja. You and I will stay together all the way to al-Aqsa, and we'll pray there, inshallah. And then we can bring you back."

"God bless you both, and God recompense you well! But I might slow you down, my girl. We may get to the

Holy City late, and then we'd have a long walk to get to the sanctuary. And I'm a tired old woman."

"May God ease our way," murmured Umm Musaab.

The Beit Fajjar intersection in the south of Bethlehem was not as choked with traffic as the driver had feared. Soldiers weren't stopping vehicles that morning, though they were still everywhere, posted behind reinforced concrete barriers that stood at intervals along each of the streets coming into the intersection. The two women found themselves with an unexpected reserve of time.

As soon as the car reached the junction that led to the crossing—at the start of Nativity Street—the driver could see a pileup of cars ahead, warning of traffic chaos across the whole area. The jam was made worse by the dozens of people who had decided to abandon their vehicles. Afraid of delay, they poured into the streets, hoping to reach the checkpoint entrance quicker on foot. It was a walk of about twenty minutes.

The women climbed out of the car before the driver could get drawn into this congestion. He continued on, down Nativity Street, toward the Bab al-Deir neighborhood. The women crossed the street and joined the other pedestrians. Umm Musaab glanced at her phone, checking the time. She had left as much as she could at home, anything with metal in it: her wristwatch, jewelry, hair clasps. Anything to reduce the possibility of triggering the metal detector and being detained. It was 8:55 a.m. They pressed on, Umm Musaab pausing whenever she got a step or two ahead, waiting until her elderly companion caught up.

Around nine fifteen, they joined a long line of people in an open-air corridor. The narrow passage stretched many meters, partially roofed by tin sheets, wire mesh running along both sides. It was no more than two meters wide. A long, slender cage. Many times, this type of crowding—often so bad that some young men would try to scramble up the wire mesh for space, and to perhaps advance a few paces ahead—had led to cases of fainting. It was especially bad for the workers who thronged into this tunnel every day, some arriving at three a.m., desperate to cross the Green Line and get to their shifts on time. People had stories of seeing death in there.

When the women joined the crowd, it must have contained nearly two hundred people. Many were blowing on their fists and rubbing their hands together for warmth. The minutes moved quickly; the line, slowly. Every few steps, the old woman's hope ascended too, as though it were the needle of some speedometer in her chest. Soon they sensed a commotion, raised voices that they couldn't quite discern, at the head of this upwardly sloping corridor. Someone shinnied halfway up the wire mesh to get a better view.

The women tried to find out what was happening, but no one had a real answer. Then it grew quiet again. The line had completely stopped moving. A few minutes later, a husband and wife who looked to be in their sixties came toward them, down the parallel corridor on the left. That path was walked by those who had been turned away, denied permission to enter Jerusalem. Someone asked the couple why the line had stopped. Frowning, the man half turned to the questioner and spoke, without slowing his pace.

"Two young fellows," he said. "They got into a fight at the *maateh* about who got to go in first. It was all a mess, and now the army is punishing everyone by stopping the line."

Hearing this, Hajja Aisha slapped her face in despair. "We'll miss the prayers now!"

"This happens all the time," said Umm Musaab, trying to calm her. "They punish folks by stopping everything, and then pretty soon they return to their posts and get back to work."

"I swear," exclaimed a woman who stood nearby, "we can never know what to expect! How they'll react, what they'll do. Like two months ago, when they shut down the crossing. As soon as people were turning back, heading to their mosques in Bethlehem after giving up on the Noble Sanctuary—well, just then, that was when they reopened it."

Hajja Aisha slapped her face again and said: "All my efforts were in vain."

"Don't lose hope in God's mercy," said Umm Musaab. "Put your trust in God."

The old woman bowed her head, putting a hand to her brow, trying to hide tears glistening in her eyes. No one said anything for a few moments.

Then Umm Musaab spoke up gently: "Hajja, I see some movement up there. It looks like they've opened the crossing again."

Hajja Aisha's hope soared. "Lord, don't let my efforts be lost," she muttered.

Now they began to inch forward. They gained a few meters each time a group made it past the turnstile. Progress felt steady. Umm Musaab said, "It's looking quicker than usual. *Rabbina yisahhil.*"

Hajja Aisha remained silent.

Over an hour after entering the line, the two women finally made it through the turnstile. People here called it the *maateh*, since it looked like the sharp implement used to pluck a slaughtered chicken's feathers. They passed a large room occupied by four soldiers in uniform, then reached a wider open space. People who had gone through the turnstile after them were overtaking them; Hajja Aisha didn't have the strength to walk so fast. Minutes later, they entered another roofed passageway. There was more room here, not such a crowd, but before long they were in another queue that doubled back on itself. Ropes guided people into single lanes that led to security gates with metal detectors.

After a slow twenty minutes, Hajja Aisha and Umm Musaab were finally facing the electronic security gate. Umm Musaab put her phone into her handbag, along with her wedding ring and a few coins. She took out a baggie, emptied it, and told Hajja Aisha to put anything containing metal into it.

"I know about this," said the old woman. "I passed through security like this at the Allenby Bridge crossing from Amman."

On a nearby counter sat several plastic bins. Umm Musaab placed her handbag and her companion's baggie into one of them, then put it on the conveyor belt connected to the security gate. She really hoped that they and their belongings would make it through. She told Hajja Aisha to go first—this way, she would still be right there, behind her, to help if the old woman triggered the alarm.

No sooner had Hajja Aisha entered the gate than the machine let out a horrid screech. Through the microphone came the raised voice of a woman with a foreign accent: *"Go back."*

Umm Musaab pulled her companion next to her. "Do you still have anything metal on you? A ring, coins, anything?"

"No, my girl, nothing. Wallahi. I put everything in the bag."

Umm Musaab inspected the old woman's hands and ears, even her hair—nothing. She gazed down at her shoes—no metal parts. She asked her to try again. When Hajja Aisha stepped forward, the piercing siren came back, followed by the army woman's outcry: *"Go back, back! Everything on the belt!"*

Hajja Aisha withdrew.

Someone in the crowd behind her spoke: "Search yourself well, Hajja. We're all late now."

Umm Musaab asked Hajja Aisha to remove her shoes. She stepped out of them and approached the gate again. This time, the alarm was silent. Umm Musaab picked up the shoes and gave them a once-over. Sure enough, there it was—a thumbtack embedded in the sole. She set the shoes onto the belt and passed the gate without issue.

They collected their belongings and continued their

journey through the checkpoint. As they walked along yet another corridor, they passed a man who was shuffling slowly as he tried to loop his belt around his trousers. They soon found themselves in a large space occupied by two partitioned cubicles. A male recruit sat in one of them, a female soldier in the other. Each had a short line of people in front of them. The two women joined the female soldier's line, and ten minutes later they reached the window. Umm Musaab told Hajja Aisha to press her identity card—which she had always been so careful to renew—up against the window; she could hopefully pass without having to get a permission document, since she was elderly. That is, if the computer didn't forbid entry, for whatever reason.

The soldier studied the ID, and then tapped something into her keyboard. She gave Hajja Aisha a curt nod to let her know that she could proceed. But the Hajja feared she might have misunderstood the nod, and so she hesitated, not wanting to provoke some sort of retribution. For a few seconds she just stood there, staring at the soldier.

The soldier said loudly, "Go in—don't you understand?" Then she said something in Hebrew that the old woman couldn't understand at all.

She passed through the gray metal barrier, and Umm Musaab followed after undergoing a similar examination. Within a few steps, they emerged into the open air. Finally, outside of those tin-roofed cages.

"I bear witness that there is no god but God . . ." Hajja Aisha murmured.

"And I bear witness that Muhammad is the messenger of God," Umm Musaab finished. "But we aren't done standing in lines. We'll probably find another at the bus."

In exactly three minutes, the pair were standing among a group of people waiting on a street that was closed off by the outer walls of the checkpoint.

"Oh Lord," Hajja Aisha said, "pray, let it all go well for us now, with no more worries." She looked around and sighed. "How much it's all changed, my dear."

"Did you know this place?" asked Umm Musaab.

"Yes. Back when things were good, we used to come here, from Hebron and the villages around, all the way to Jerusalem through Bethlehem, and then back the same way. On the Hebron bus. This crossing business didn't exist, *crossing* that these soldiers, this army, use to divide Bethlehem and Jerusalem. There was no *crossing*, as we know it now."

"Yes. I remember those days too, Hajja."

There was a ripple of movement. "The bus is coming," someone called out.

The driver had to back up into the closed-off street as the crowd surged forward. Umm Musaab stayed where she was, close to Hajja Aisha who was not strong enough to compete with the jostling crowd. But as chance had it, the bus stopped and opened its door directly in front of her. These travel companions were the first to get in.

When the bus moved off, Hajja Aisha was peering through the window. "Ay, my goodness, it has all changed completely!"

"What makes you say that?"

"Those strange buildings you see, over on the right? Well, before, they weren't there. Up there on the heights people called Jabel Abu Ghneim. And not those to the left either, that's what people call is-Salib. Ay! They aren't using the crossing just to separate the folks in Bethlehem from the folks in Jerusalem, my girl."

"Do you know the names of all the places around here, Hajja? You talk as if you're a native of Bethlehem."

Hajja Aisha didn't respond immediately. She stared at a monastery the bus was approaching. "Yes . . . I know some of them, anyway. Mar Elias Monastery over there. My father and I would visit it when I was little—yes, we came here to work. During olive-picking season. The road was easy—it was all open. There was none of this cursed *crossing* business. Sometimes, we even arrived before the local folks did. The Greek monk who managed the olive groves—we called him al-Khuri—he used to tell those latecomers, *Just look at this man! He comes all the way from Hebron and he's here before you are. Because he wants to stay alive.*"

The bus stopped at Musrara, a stone's throw from the main entrance into the walled Old City of Jerusalem— the Damascus Gate. In their everyday language, people called it Bab al-Amud, "Gate of the Column." The passengers poured out. Most were clearly off to pray, hurrying toward Bab al-Amud.

Hajja Aisha heard one man say to his companion, "Hurry up, now! The call to prayer must have been a few minutes ago."

She turned to Umm Musaab. "The call to prayer—already?"

"Yes . . . I didn't want to let you know. May God give us strength!"

"My dear, you go on ahead. It's not your fault you aren't there yet! I'll just keep walking with the others who are late. So many people, we're not the only ones delayed by these crossings."

"Oh no, Hajja, I won't leave you. We'll get there in enough time, inshallah. There's the whole Friday sermon. As long as we get there before that ends . . ."

They reached the steps leading down to Bab al-Amud. Happening to glance to the right, Hajja Aisha saw some soldiers stopping a group of young men. A woman was standing a few strides away. One soldier walked up to her and began scolding her.

"No, I won't leave!" she responded. "Why have you stopped my boy? He hasn't done anything. None of these boys have, they were just walking through. I want my son!"

Umm Musaab heard the Hajja mutter something, but didn't catch it. She sensed the older woman's anxiety. "We see this a lot, she said. It's just an ordinary thing here."

Hajja Aisha peered up at the Jerusalem wall, a sight she hadn't seen in years. Her eyes fell on a young soldier, commanding the famous lookout at the top of Bab al-Amud, holding his gun. She jerked her head toward him and spoke to her companion: "And this devil? What's he doing there?"

"From where he is, he can see everything that moves, everywhere around here."

They went through the enormous gate, reaching the junction—in one direction was the Khan al-Zeit Market, and in the other al-Wad Street, the main route to the sacred mosque precinct. Vendors stood behind stalls stocked with the famous al-Quds bread covered with sesame, peasant women were selling an array of fruits and vegetables. Some of them were trying to flag down worshippers but found little success, since the mosque-goers were anxious to pray before it was too late.

The two women headed down al-Wad Street. Hajja Aisha was clearly tired out; she looked fragile. Before they reached the next junction in front of the Austrian hospice, they heard the hot whistle of bullets.

Umm Musaab was several steps ahead, but she caught Hajja Aisha's exclamation. "Oh Lord! That's close by."

Crowds rushed toward them, heading back to Bab al-Amud. Some, however, tried to escape the danger by continuing on to the al-Aqsa Mosque, hoping to slip inside amid the commotion, before the soldiers closed the road entirely. The two women found themselves in this wave of people. The troops brandished their rifles in all directions, attempting to block the hospice junction.

Hajja Aisha veered toward the shop fronts to her right. She kept stumbling along, seeming to pay little attention to what was going on around her. Umm Musaab followed her, and as they drew parallel with the junction itself, they couldn't resist the tug of curiosity. What was causing all this mayhem? They gazed to the left and got their answer: a dark-skinned youth of twenty or so sprawled on the ground, in the Via Dolorosa. Blood streamed from him, breaking into tributaries. A soldier kicked his arms open until they were level with his shoulders and his body took the form of a blood-splattered cross.

The old woman felt a tremor pass through her, racking her entire body. "God help his poor mother," she said in a low, hoarse voice.

Umm Musaab burst into tears. "God, this is wrong! *Hasbunallah wa ni'mal wakil*. Oh God . . ."

They kept moving, pushed along by the crowd.

The muezzin was announcing the prayers, and as they reached Bab al-Majlis, one of the gates into the mosque, people began dropping to the ground to pray. Those who were farther back in the crowd could not make their way in due to the rows of believers that had formed just inside the doorway. Others could not enter because soldiers had snatched their IDs and then turned them away. People clustered where they were, ready to pray in the narrow space outside the entrance. There were three rows—two of men, and one of women behind them. No one seemed concerned anymore about the gathering soldiers. Hajja Aisha found herself on one end of the women's row, to the right, while Umm Musaab had somehow ended up on the other end, near the gate.

Praise be to God, Hajja Aisha said to herself as the prayers began. *God helped me be here for prayers in the Noble Sanctuary, even if just at the door. After this, I can go inside to visit the mosque properly, and I'll pray in the Well of Souls.*

Once the imam and worshippers finished praying, the courtyard of the Noble Sanctuary erupted with the sounds of bullets and tear gas and shouting.

"With our souls!" someone yelled. "We'll give our lives for you, our martyr, we'll give with blood!"

Those who were praying outside tried to crowd into the mosque courtyard. Some of them shoved their way in before the soldiers managed to close the gate. The doors shut right in front of Hajja Aisha, while Umm Musaab was propelled inside by the crowd. The old woman saw her companion shouting to her from inside. In the hubbub, it was impossible to hear anything being said.

Only seconds later, a strange and very strong smell assaulted Hajja Aisha's nose. She felt it more than smelled it, like a spray of hot pepper. Heavy smoke hung in the air and filled her chest. She could feel the danger to her weak heart. She knew that she had to get away from here. She began coughing, and her eyes were stinging. Tears ran down her cheeks. Reaching the junction, the old woman turned back for a moment to look at the gates into the Noble Sanctuary. A holy, inviolable space. She was sobbing and gasping, choking from the gas, as she tried to retrace her steps, back toward Bab al-Amud.

MOSQUES, CHURCHES, FALAFEL, MUJADDARA

BY JAMEEL AL-SALHOUT

American Colony Hotel

Translated by Roger Allen

Stephanie arrived at the American Colony Hotel and found Khalil waiting in the lounge. He had arrived a few minutes earlier. She gave him a loving hug, and noticed how much he'd changed since the last time they met. Khalil refused to register his name with the reception clerk. He rolled Stephanie's suitcase into the room she'd booked them.

Stephanie asked, "Do you like the smell of my sweat as much as I like yours?"

"For sure!" Khalil responded.

She stretched out on the bed; her suntanned body looked like the skin of a fish. That was tempting for Khalil: in that moment his lover resembled a sea nymph. He smiled, because he wasn't sure if those creatures were real or ancient fairy tale. Nevertheless, it was nice.

Stephanie had feared that he might be put off by her, but his warm greeting made her happy; he had stroked her body from head to toe.

"Do you still find me beautiful now that you've gotten to know me?" she asked.

"Yes, I find you beautiful all over again."

Khalil stretched out beside her. He recalled a story one of the town elders had told him, about a young man who spotted a woman in a shiny dress standing on a hill. He started toward her, growing more eager the closer he got. She noticed and covered her mouth with her scarf, feigning shyness. His approach made her happy, because she knew him. She thought that he knew her too. The gleam in her eyes looked like piercing arrows to him. He quickened his pace until he was standing beside her. He greeted her, and she answered by removing the scarf and flashing a broad smile. It was poor Rummana, with her harelip and inherited snub nose. Shocked, he made his way back, cursing her all the while.

It's a waste for someone like you to wear a dress like that! the young man yelled.

It's a sin for anyone like you to see what's under it, she replied maliciously.

Stephanie had left the bathroom door open while she took a cold shower. "Were you talking to yourself?" she asked.

"I was thinking about what happened when we first met," Khalil said.

"But you were shivering with fright when we first met."

"Every beginning is hard . . . but it was an unforgettable meeting."

"Of course. First fruits always taste delicious."

She put on slacks and a long-sleeve blouse, not wanting to show her sunburned skin from the Dead Sea. She sat down on a chair beside the bed and noticed how drowsy he looked.

"Do you want to go to sleep?" she asked.

"No, no, it's just a lazy feeling. A cold shower will get rid of it."

Once he had taken the shower, his energy returned. He sat next to her on the bed.

"I have to go back to London before the week's over," she said. "I've reserved a ticket for Thursday. The doctors have decided to operate on my mother to remove a gallstone. She called and asked me to be with her. She's scared of surgery."

"I hope she recovers quickly," Khalil said.

He was upset that she had agreed to go, but tried to avoid thinking about it. And despite how he felt, he gave in when she insisted on seeing his home. He called his friend George, asking him to give them a ride. George said he would be there in the evening.

Khalil's father was sitting in front of the hair tent with his two wives. So were Khalil's brothers, Kamil and Salih. Two hours earlier a ewe had given birth. She kept bleating and sniffing her newborn with affection, while the lamb cried faintly as it searched for its mother's teats. Stephanie was thrilled to see the pair. She picked up the lamb, brought it to her chest, and cuddled it. The ewe bleated, demanding her baby back, so Stephanie returned it. She shook hands with Khalil's family and sat down on a small wooden chair, nodding and smiling as Khalil introduced them all.

He pointed at the stone house. "That's our home. As I told you, it's modest."

She gestured at the hair tent. "This is lovely. I wish I had one like it."

George translated for Khalil's father.

"By God," the old man said, "may the angel of death set eyes on you! Where have you brought this despicable woman from?"

"She's a British journalist," George said. "She interviewed Khalil about prison conditions. She insisted on seeing his home."

"Were you born here, Khalil?" Stephanie asked.

"No, I was born in my maternal grandfather's cave."

"Ah, let's visit it to take some pictures!"

"It's far from here, and inaccessible by car. We'd need to walk through the desert for two hours to get there."

"Amazing, terrific! It's our chance to walk in the open air, in nature, away from the noise of the city."

George did his best to back Khalil: "The cave's in a military zone that's been closed since before the occupation."

"Why?" Stephanie asked.

"They have regulations that enable them to close any area for army use."

"But that's illegal."

"Is there such a thing as *legal* occupation?" George asked.

Salih's mother brought a bowl of tea.

"Where do you sleep, Khalil?" Stephanie asked.

"Sometimes I sleep out here under the fig tree, or in the hair tent, or just in my room."

"You're so lucky! Getting to sleep in nature's arms . . . Can I sleep here under the fig tree?" She looked up at the sky. "I'd love to count the stars and follow their course."

Khalil and George chuckled.

"What did that glossy serpent girl say to make you both laugh?" Khalil's father asked.

"She wants to sleep under the fig tree," Khalil said.

"Good heavens above." The patriarch shook his head. "How come you've brought us this disaster?"

"Tell her it's fine," Kamil said with a laugh. "We'll lay out a blanket for her and Khalil under the tree."

"You're *not* translating that," their father said, then turned to Kamil. "That's wrong, I don't want to hear it from you again. You seem to be treating people's honor as some kind of joke."

"You have beautiful weather here," Stephanie said. "People can sleep in the fields. London's climate is very different. There's fog everywhere, and it can rain without warning."

"Customs here don't allow women to sleep outside the home," George explained. "Men feel afraid for them."

Stephanie was astonished. "Afraid? Afraid of what? Why aren't they afraid for themselves?"

"They're scared of wild beasts," Khalil chimed in.

Stephanie's eyes lit up. "Do wild animals come out here? It's a great opportunity to observe them in their natural habitat! Don't worry about me; I know how to deal with them. In Africa, I've seen tigers, leopards, lions, elephants, hyenas, foxes, gazelles, and wild cows. They're a wonderful sight!"

"Heaven help us!" Khalil exclaimed to the others. "Who'll get us out of this mess?"

"Forget this nonsense," said his father. "George, you're

our guest. Whad'ya say we butcher a lamb? We'll roast it and have ourselves a good time tonight."

"What's he saying?" Stephanie asked.

"He wants to butcher a lamb for you," George said. "They'll roast it on a spit."

"Who's going to kill it?"

George pointed at Kamil.

"He'll be using a knife to kill it right in front of us?" She sounded upset. "That's dreadful! I can't stand the sight of blood."

Khalil asked George to take Stephanie back to the hotel. "Get us out of this fiasco. She seems happy to have seen how miserable our life is."

"What do you mean *miserable?*" George said. "This is the environment we're losing. She's happy because she never sees anything like it in her own country." He turned to Stephanie. "What do you say we leave now? Come on, I'll take you back to the hotel."

"Let's go, Khalil!" she said.

"I'll catch up with you in the morning," Khalil replied. "I can't go with you now."

"Why not?"

He spoke quietly: "I don't want them all to realize that we're in some kind of relationship. Our customs don't allow for that."

"Are you *afraid* of them? Who are you afraid of? Your father? Are they crazy? Why won't they let you live your life? You're not a child anymore." She looked at the tree. "Or is it that you want to watch the stars by yourself?"

"I'll explain everything tomorrow."

* * *

From the top of Jabel Mukaber, in the direction of Baq'a, Stephanie spotted the Old City of Jerusalem, a shining jewel, adorned with the golden Dome of the Rock whose rays of light illuminated the East. She asked George to stop the car, and they both stepped out. The sheer magic of the Holy City compelled her to sit on the ground. She took lots of photographs. She captured the village of Silwan, which sloped down from Ras al-Amud to the Kidron Valley. Then she snapped the western slope of the Mount of Olives, ending at the Church of All Nations, next to Gethsemane. Stephanie wanted to spend the night there, but George couldn't wait any longer; his wife was expecting him.

At the hotel, Stephanie invited George to have a glass of whiskey with her, but he declined and left. She sat in the lounge. It was too early for bed, so she ordered a beer, drank it, and then ordered another. She was disappointed in Khalil. She loved him, longed for him. She had come from London to meet him. How could he leave her on her own? Why did he not want to be with her tonight? She couldn't fathom what he had meant by *customs*. She wondered about the hold that families had over their children in this country. Did people here fear relationships between men and women, or was it that such relations had to be confined to marriage? She kept sipping her beer and ruminating. Just five nights to go before she would be leaving this puzzling country. It was beautiful and holy, but also suffered from wars and other terrible problems. People's customs were peculiar. She remembered how her

Indian boyfriend used to hug and kiss her in front of his family. They had not objected. Far from it, they had been very happy, even though, like the Arabs, they were Orientals. The comparison bothered her . . . If not their culture, she at least admired Arab machismo, she concluded.

That night, Khalil was also feeling unhappy about his relationship with Stephanie. He regarded her as a playgirl, with no goal in life other than using her wealth to sate her desires. He spent the night contemplating his future plans.

Stephanie woke to the sound of Khalil's gentle knocking. She opened the door and stood there yawning in her nightdress, smelling of alcohol. He hugged and kissed her.

"When you're drowsy," he said, "you're even more fascinating and beautiful."

"Do you really mean that?" she asked.

"Certainly! Any woman who can look beautiful in the morning before she's put on her makeup is truly beautiful. It's the kind of natural beauty that men want."

She threw herself down on the bed in a display of undisguised flirtation, and told him off for not spending the previous night with her.

He sighed. "You need to understand that there are cultural differences between peoples. Jerusalem isn't London."

They went out to tour the Old City. They passed by the Damascus Gate, the Khan al-Zeit Market, and spice stalls. Next they browsed the al-Bashura Market.

By the Chain Gate, most of the businesses had been converted into tourist shops. They attracted Jews on their way to pray at the Buraq Wall, also called the Wailing Wall, the western border of the al-Aqsa Mosque. Guards stopped Stephanie at the mosque's entrance. Tourists had to go in through the Council Gate, they told her. So Khalil brought her around to the al-Wad Market. They took a break by the Hammam al-Ayn, an ancient bathhouse that was unexpectedly closed. Then they walked toward the Council Gate.

Khalil bought a shabby Palestinian kaffiyeh for Stephanie to cover her head. They paused in the al-Aqsa courtyard, at a loss as to where to begin. The site had a power to it, a history that announced its own magnitude. Stephanie indicated the Dome of the Rock, so they approached it.

Khalil stopped and told her about the mighty Temple Mount. "As you can see, the al-Aqsa compound consists of several buildings, with a number of important features. These grounds contain four minarets, twenty-five wells, a pool for ritual cleansing, and several benches that were created for scholars, Sufis, and foreigners. Here we have the Domes of the Chain, the Ascension, and the Prophet. And, of course, the Dome of the Rock sits in the middle." He pointed at the golden shrine. "The compound can be accessed through eleven open gates. There are seven porticoes in all: one in the middle, three on the east side, and three on the west. They are raised on fifty-three marble columns and forty-nine stone pillars. Of all the porticoes, the most important is the one opposite the Gate of Honor of the Prophets; it extends from the Chain Gate to the Moroccan Gate, and holds two sundials for timing prayers."

In front of the mosque, Khalil took Stephanie's camera and asked her to stay right where she was. He directed her hand so it looked as though she were holding the Dome of the Rock, then snapped a photo. A passerby was kind enough to photograph both of them in the same spot. Stephanie took dozens of pictures of the mosque, inside and out, and the monuments in the courtyard. Once the muezzin announced the noon prayer, they left the compound through the Chain Gate.

Upon exiting, they were stopped by two Israeli border guards who wanted to check Stephanie's ID. Undoubtedly they thought she was a young Israeli woman going out with an Arab. Their English was terrible. When they saw her British passport, they let the two of them go, but only after Stephanie had yelled at them.

"Good for you, lover boy!" one of the guards said in poor Arabic.

Khalil pointed to a building behind the guards. "This is part of the Tankiziyya. Inside there's an ancient mosaic prayer niche as high as the Buraq Wall. In the Jordanian period, it was used as an Islamic religious school. Its upper floor held the offices of the Islamic Conference. The occupation forces took it over and stopped students from entering."

Close by, Khalil pointed out the Khalidi Library. "This historic library was founded in 1899 by Raghib al-Khalidi, of the prominent Jerusalem Khalidi family. The collection features numerous manuscripts, rare books, newspapers, and journals, in various languages. Individual Khalidis contributed their personal libraries."

Continuing, the pair encountered a falafel vendor; the aroma was filling the entire market. Stephanie was hungry, so Khalil bought falafel sandwiches for both of them, handing the vendor ten Israeli liroth.

"Keep the change," Stephanie said in English, then promptly wolfed down her sandwich. "That's very tasty."

"Tomorrow morning," Khalil said, "we'll have hummus and falafel for breakfast."

"There's no city in the world like Jerusalem. How I wish I could visit everywhere . . ."

"You'd need a whole year for that! But you can look down on the whole city from a special elevated spot."

Khalil now took her to the Christian Quarter, to the Lutheran Church of the Redeemer, famous for its tall tower overlooking the entire Old City.

They admired the church for a while, then climbed the tower. The ancient city looked like a mosaic—difficult to describe, but alluring. Stephanie's gaze fell on the settlements that had been built to the west of the Buraq Wall. To her, they did not match the aesthetics. She asked about them.

Khalil let out a heavy sigh. "Israel established those by demolishing old quarters, before the sound of gunfire had ceased in the Six-Day War in 1967. They demolished 1,012 historic buildings, including mosques and schools, and kicked out their Palestinian owners. All for the sake of building those utterly inappropriate structures and creating a Jewish settlers' quarter in the heart of the Old City."

"It's incredibly sad that they destroyed human civilization here," Stephanie said.

"That's quite normal for them. Their idea of civilization is based on power, killing, and destruction."

After taking numerous photos in every direction, Stephanie asked about the dividing line between East and West Jerusalem.

Khalil pointed west. "Old City is part of East Jerusalem, which was occupied during the June 1967 war. West Jerusalem lies outside the city walls on the west side."

Stephanie peered at West Jerusalem and pointed to some old buildings. "Those look Arabic," she said.

"That's right. They're Arab houses. Their occupants were expelled during the Nakba, the mass expulsions of 1948. Jewish settlers live there now."

"Where were the Arab owners expelled to?"

"All over the globe . . . although the majority of Palestinian refugees now live in camps on the West Bank, in Gaza, and in various Arab countries."

Khalil suggested that they leave the Old City through the Jaffa Gate and make a circuit of the walls. Stephanie agreed. After they passed the Jaffa Gate, she turned around and took another picture.

"Do you see how this gate looks different from all the others?" Khalil didn't give her time to respond. "It was built and decorated just like the others. But then Emperor Wilhelm II of Germany visited in October 1898, to perform the pilgrimage and dedicate the Church of the Redeemer. The plan was for him to enter the city on a splendid horse-drawn carriage. But the gate was not wide enough, so they demolished part of the nearby wall." He pointed to a breach through which vehicles could pass.

"That's why things here look out of proportion. Just one of the many criminal acts committed on the city's historic wall."

They walked north toward the hotel. They passed through the New Gate, so called because it was relatively new, completed in 1889. Ottoman sultan Abdülhamīd II authorized its construction to form a connection between the Christian Quarter and European Christian institutions outside the wall.

"You get the impression," Khalil commented with a laugh, "that the presence of Europeans has afflicted the city wall."

They spent the night at the American Colony Hotel.

Late that night, Stephanie recalled her very first meeting with Khalil, in London: "You were just fourteen then. It's good for a girl to begin a relationship with a completely inexperienced, gullible young man. She's breaking down the impact of aggressive masculinity. I was thrilled when your shyness made you pour with sweat. But do you realize . . ." She paused. "If the police had found out what I'd done to you, they would have arrested me and charged me with assaulting a minor. Even my mother asked me how old you were! I used the fact that you were so tall to lie to her and say you were twenty. My mother said that your face made you look like a child."

Back then, Khalil had not realized that a boy of fourteen was still considered a child. In his village, boys that age got married. Some girls would do so even younger. And yet he was happy to discover the female world at such an age.

* * *

The next morning, Khalil took Stephanie to a popular restaurant on Saladin Street for breakfast—hummus and falafel. She watched how other diners dipped their bites in hummus, copying them. She couldn't get over how delicious the food was.

"It's our national dish," Khalil said, "the main meal for poor people at restaurants."

His remark surprised Stephanie. "If this is for poor people, then what do the rich eat? Don't they eat this delicious food as well?"

"For rich people, this is a secondary consideration." Khalil laughed. "They make it an appetizer for the main course."

"What's the main course for poor people?"

"Poor people eat what they can get. They don't fuss about appetizers and main courses. All they're worried about is filling their hungry bellies."

"Eastern cuisine is wonderful," Stephanie said. "I love Eastern dishes. Indian food's delicious too, but it relies a lot on hot spices."

They left the restaurant and walked slowly toward the Damascus Gate, heading for the Church of the Holy Sepulchre. Stephanie took in all the beautiful sights as they passed through the Khan al-Zeit Market. She caught a fragrant waft of coffee, and Khalil assured her that they'd stop at a café later.

In front of the church, Khalil began his monologue: "It was built over Golgotha, the site where the Messiah was crucified. It's regarded as the holiest, most important

Christian church. According to belief, the church contains the place where Jesus—peace be upon him!—was buried: the Holy Sepulchre. It is also called the Church of the Resurrection in reference to Jesus's rising on the third day.

"The church's construction was supervised by Queen Helena, the mother of Constantine the Great. It lasted from 326 CE to 335 CE. The keys to the church are kept by two ancient Muslim families: one family is the official custodian of the keys, the other serves as doorkeeper. They have held the keys since the twelfth century because of disputes between Christian denominations.

"At the very bottom of Golgotha hill there is an illuminated glass window, and an earthquake meter. Some Christians believe that the church is also the site where Adam, the first human, was buried. Another reason why it is so important."

They entered. Stephanie genuflected before Jesus's holy tomb. She said her prayers with her hands on her chest, then made the sign of the cross. After exploring inside, they headed back to the Damascus Gate and caught a taxi to the Church of the Nativity in Bethlehem, where Jesus was born.

Later, Stephanie asked, "What other popular dishes do you have besides hummus and falafel?"

"We have a lot," Khalil said.

"Which ones do you like?"

"Mujaddara and maftoul."

"Then let's try them both for dinner."

"You can't get them in restaurants. Women cook them at home, nowhere else."

"Can we eat them in your home?"

This woman once again baffled Khalil. Now that he had tied himself in knots by calling those his favorite dishes, how could he refuse her request? He got in touch with George.

"I need you to do something for me, dear friend," Khalil told him. "Please. That heathen woman Stephanie wants to eat some mujaddara and maftoul. Please drive to my house and ask my mother to make one of them for dinner."

"Don't worry, Khalil, I'll ask my wife to make mujaddara. You two can dine with us."

Khalil was delighted. This would save him from having to explain anything to his parents.

At sunset, Khalil and Stephanie set out for George's house in the Christian Quarter. They stopped at a café by the entrance to the Khan al-Zeit Market, sitting on small wooden chairs as they sipped their Arabic coffee. The gazes of passersby and café regulars kept probing Stephanie's body. She asked Khalil if they were staring because she was a foreigner. Khalil replied that he had no idea, though in his own mind he attributed it to suppression and sexual frustration. Many of them believed it was easy to get what you wanted from foreign women.

George and his wife and mother welcomed them. They seated Khalil and Stephanie before bringing in refreshments: a bottle of whiskey, another of arak, five beers, a bucket of ice, and three bowls—one with pistachios, another with almonds, and the third with slices of tomatoes and cucumbers. George asked them both what they would like to drink.

"I'll start with some beer," Stephanie said. "But then I'll have some whiskey."

George opened a bottle of beer, poured some of it into a glass, and handed it to Stephanie. He did the same for Khalil. Salwa, his wife, drank one straight from the bottle. She offered another to her mother-in-law.

Stephanie raised her glass. "To your health!"

Everyone held up their drinks in a toast.

Then they started their mujaddara dinner. Stephanie had trouble pronouncing the word, so George wrote it out for her. She sampled it from the tip of her fork before taking a full bite. It was delicious. When she asked about maftoul, Salwa told her about it.

"Khalil's mother is really good at preparing it," Salwa said.

Khalil nodded. "Tomorrow, we'll have some in our house at noontime." He invited George and his family to join them.

The following morning, Khalil woke up at six and got dressed. He left the hotel room as quietly as possible so as not to wake Stephanie, and took a cab from the Damascus Gate to his home. His parents were sitting in the hair tent. Khalil explained that the English journalist was eager to try some maftoul. He would be bringing her to eat it for lunch. George, his wife, and his mother would be coming as well.

Back at the American Colony Hotel, Khalil opened the door quietly. Stephanie was still asleep. But when he stretched out beside her, she opened her eyes and smiled, putting her hand on his chest. He rolled over and kissed her, and they both melted into the firmament of passion. After a while they got up and took a shower together.

"You're going to miss these encounters of ours, Khalil. I'm leaving in less than twenty-eight hours."

"Are you going to miss them too?"

"Don't worry about me." She laughed. "I'll work things out."

She suggested that they have hummus and falafel for breakfast. Khalil, in turn, proposed that they make another circuit of Jerusalem's historic wall after eating.

Khalil took her to a local restaurant some twenty meters from Herod's Gate inside the Old City. It ran more smoothly and was cleaner than the one on Saladin Street.

"So what do people who don't go to restaurants eat?" Stephanie asked.

"Cheese, yogurt, olives and olive oil, and thyme."

"What's thyme?"

"A wild plant that gets picked in springtime. People dry it, then grind it like coffee. They dip their food in oil and thyme."

"Can I taste it?"

"Of course."

Khalil asked the waiter to bring a small bowl of oil and a bit of thyme. He dipped a piece of falafel in both, then took a bite.

"That's how we eat it," he told Stephanie.

She tried and liked it, then said, "I'm thinking of opening a restaurant with Arab food in London."

"That's a great idea. But you'd need an Arab cook who's good at making these dishes."

"That's easy. Once British people get a taste, they'll keep coming back, and the business will flourish. It'll make huge profits!"

After their meal, Khalil purchased two bottles of cold water from the grocer next door. They went out through Herod's Gate and ambled along. Stephanie kept taking photographs.

They entered a Muslim cemetery. Khalil pointed to the tomb of the unknown soldier, commemorating the martyrs of the Jordanian Armed Forces who fell defending the Old City in the June 1967 war. He stood humbly before the tomb and recited the Fatiha for their souls. They carried on walking.

In front of the Lion's Gate, Stephanie noticed two lions carved into the stone. She asked Khalil about them. He explained that they symbolized the heroic acts of those who had defended, and continued to defend, the city.

As they proceeded through the second half of the cemetery, Khalil pointed out the Golden Gate, by which were buried two noble companions of Muhammad, ʻUbadah Ibn al-Samit and Shadad Ibn Aus, who took part in the Islamic conquest of the city.

At the end of their walk, they sat down on a hill. Stephanie gazed at the Church of All Nations.

"That church," Khalil began, "was built over the bedrock where it is believed the Messiah prayed and wept before his arrest. The first church built on the site goes back to the fourth century, during the Byzantine era. The Persians destroyed it when they invaded Palestine, but the Franks rebuilt it in the twelfth century during their occupation of the Holy City. The current church, considered one of the most beautiful in the Holy Land, was built in 1924. Many countries jointly funded it, and, for that reason it's known as the Church of All Nations. Its garden has eight olive trees from the Roman era. The striking mosaic on the façade remains ever vibrant . . . It is from this church that the Way of the Cross begins, which, according to Christian belief, is the road that the Messiah took—in fourteen stations—on the way to Golgotha." Khalil listed the stations.

Stephanie admired the church's beauty even though she knew so little about its history. Once again she pulled out her camera.

The day was only half over, yet the sun was directly overhead. Khalil and Stephanie were sweaty and exhausted. They rode a taxi to his family's home in Jabel Mukaber. Khalil's father welcomed them. Both his wives gave Stephanie a hug and a kiss, and she laughed at this unusual gesture.

"In our country," Khalil said, "women kiss other women they know."

"Why don't they kiss the men?" Stephanie asked.

"They can only kiss specific men."

"Your country's beautiful and holy, your food's delicious, but your culture's weird!"

George arrived with his family. While he, his mother, and Salwa were being welcomed, Stephanie caught hold of George's little boy, gave him a hug, and spoke to him. His name was Zainab. He smiled as though he knew her and understood what she was saying.

For Stephanie they prepared a plate of maftoul with local turkey breast on top. Another plate, with meat and broth, was placed in front of her and Zainab. Everyone else gathered around the mansaf.

"What's that dish?" Stephanie asked.

"This is maftoul," Zainab replied, "and that's mansaf."

Stephanie tasted the maftoul and found it delicious. "I'll only eat the maftoul and a piece of chicken. I don't eat lamb."

"Taste it," Zainab said, "it's wonderful."

But Stephanie refused. "I'm only used to eating beef."

CHECKPOINTS OF DEATH

BY NUZHA AL-RAMLAWI

Qalandia Checkpoint

Translated by Catherine Cobham

Today was like any other day, noise and confusion raging over the checkpoints. Rita, arriving from her night of exile, hoping to see the city, was tired of standing in front of closed barriers. She walked over the new pedestrian bridge at the Qalandia checkpoint. Eyes looked hollow in weary faces. People leaned on their pain and walked through their suffering, the distance stretching ahead of them.

As Rita contemplated the passersby, she was struck by her own challenges. She screamed inwardly: *I will get through my sadness and weariness and I will win!* The wheels of sorrow had crushed her hopes of returning, but now that she was back she felt no relief from the hardship of exile or the fragility gnawing at her bones. She looked like a tortoise making its slow way over the bridge of misery. At a distance, she saw a familiar face. Eyes met, and a tape of old memories leaped out of school doors and played in front of her. Souls embraced once more.

Amani, who lived in front of the wall on the city side, crossed the checkpoint and began questioning her: "You're Rita, aren't you, daughter of our neighbor Umm Jarees, my childhood friend and schoolmate?"

Rita smiled and went on looking at Amani's lips to be sure she'd understood. "Yes, I'm Rita, in flesh and blood!"

"How are you, dear Rita?"

"Sorry, raise your voice when you speak." She tapped her ear. "The battery in my hearing aid is dead and I can't hear anything."

"All this chaos around you, the shrieking, the hooting, the vehicles—you can't hear it?"

"I can only hear a humming noise and distorted sounds."

"Okay, I'll raise my voice and come closer to your ear." She shifted forward. "How are you? When did you return from America?"

"I came home as a tourist. I lost my Jerusalem ID card because I was away for so long and couldn't return in time."

"May God help you bear the misery of exile and the misery of staying here."

"My dear, I hope to pass the rest of my life walking the streets of my homeland."

Rita was amazed by what she saw around her. "I can see a wall and gates blocking our entry to the city. And what is this long bridge that twists and turns, like a snake lying in wait to crush us?"

It has many objectives, my friend. Although years have passed, our pain has not subsided. Seasons of displacement have come one after another, followed by seasons of Judaization. We have had failed treaties that destroyed, divided, cut, and joined. The wall is the same age as the severed homeland. It cut through the city and divided the divided, a demon that arose to demolish our dreams, drive away our sea, disperse our people. It continues to kill our hopes. It has extinguished the joys and freedom of our city, mangled its unity, and devoured its spaces. Whatever stands in its way will be uprooted.

Hearing this increases the pain in my feet that I was already feeling on this hateful bridge. How sad it is! The city's features have changed. Where are the mountains covered with crops and olive trees, the wide streets? I see skyscrapers that hide the light. I'd always dreamed of returning during my exile . . . but now my dreams are dying in a sea of racism.

The wall is as long as the sorrow in our hearts. Soldiers came to this land without being asked. They uprooted its trees and built settlements on the roots. They blew up houses without mercy; bulldozers created clouds of sand and mountains of rubble. Hands in chains are incapable of embracing places. The eyes of the defeated resist expressions of pain, making sure their fear does not show.

O God, what am I hearing about my city? I still feel like a child whose braids rest on the steps of the ancient archways, whose footsteps play with shadows in the alleys. I'm still in love with its squares and courtyards. Our voices continue to sing in temples on feast days, and rise among the colonnades of the mosques. In my exile, homesickness lit lamps in the corners of my memory, where the prayers of worshippers and the hymns of the thankful rise in the air, the voices of street vendors parading their wares . . . We dance, run here and there with the boys, launch paper airplanes in the wind so that they rise into the clouds. We run until the distances vanish behind us . . . O God, how beautiful our city is!

Our city was still breathing, some of its buildings leveled to the ground, the wretched folk racing to inspect the rubble of their homes. They searched for memories, images, digging deep, but their hopes were in vain. The bulldozers mangled the letters children had written on the walls and destroyed the innocence in their tearful eyes. They laughed and drew hope as wide as the sky, inspired by the tumult of speeches and celebrations. They shouted in resistance, but the world was ashamed to wake up.

Babies' voices were lost in the crowd, their little breaths stopping under the sun of waiting. They still wriggled and cried, and patient mothers painted joy from sorrow and wove smiles from pain. The infants didn't care and carried on crying, searching for their bottles in the crowd of people waiting.

"Do you remember our school trips to the sea?" Rita asked. "Do you remember the day we made our big dream houses out of sand? The waves took them far away."

"Who could forget, my friend? My God, we're tired of standing here. There's nothing to be gained from calling out. The people waiting are all in despair like us. Now they're knocking on the closed gates. Listen . . . their voices are growing louder. The people are rising up again. They've emerged from the womb of survival and taken root in this place."

The soldiers didn't care. They fired a hail of bullets to silence the voices.

Rita peered at Amani and said, "God . . . what I see is so ugly. Look at the people's faces. They're so full of pain and anger, just like the city."

"How can it not be sad when loved ones are absent

and brothers separated? They are stranded, unable to enter the city. The wall has changed its face, falsified its history, torn off its limbs. How cruel these occupiers are! Look closely at the faces of those waiting, their eyes sunken from the pain of standing. These damned checkpoints make them suffer. Their voices sound desperate, stifled, yet still they shout." Amani exhaled and kept her eyes fixed on the people pleading to be allowed to cross.

They finally reached the end of the bridge. Tired, they sat on a rock facing the wall, waiting like the others. In her dreams, Rita had been heading toward prayers and love. But now, when the gates were opened, she was not allowed to cross. She shouted, "If I can stay alive, I will tear up all your checkpoints and return to the city!" She wept for a long time, resting her head against the closed gates, and waved from a distance at the people crossing. She looked contemptuously at the barrier and felt her soul passing it and embracing the walls of the Old City.

She sat down again and thought of students crossing to and from school, and workers who crossed daily—the long hours, the dangers. In the faces at the checkpoint, she read tales of weariness; in the chaos of congested vehicles, she heard groans and sighs but no words. She sat, sharing the pain of waiting with them, and in her heart she cried out, *Open the gates for me, just for an hour! Let me see lamplight spilling from a corner of our old house, and then I'll come back!*

Some who waited around her disappeared and began ascending and descending winding roads. Long distances would wear them down and bring them up against other checkpoints. Hope would fade and misery would flourish in a large waiting room overflowing with suffering people. Their bags and bodies would be searched and put through metal-detecting gates. They would try to arrive on time but would always be late.

Rita said goodbye to Amani and moved off. Those waiting doggedly in front of the gates saw that Rita had lost her way. She took a route where there were no stop signs or warnings: all she could see was empty space, tears blurring her vision.

From a distance, Amani called out, "Rita, sweetheart, stop—don't go any farther! Don't cross the line. Please come back. The birds of oblivion will take you and fly away, leaving memory behind. I'm begging you! Don't take another step into the labyrinth. Don't leave the checkpoint unless you have won. The foxes don't play fair, Rita. Don't go near them, please. Don't leave your innocent blood on the sidewalks. There is no blood money for you in the traditions of these cowards, no retribution or justice with strangers . . . We are tired and suffering to the marrow of our bones."

Walking on sadly, Rita became a stranger to place and time. The soldiers observed her movements and restrained her gentle steps, so she stood still. The bullets descended on her exhausted body. Angry eyes observed the sacrificial lamb. The gates opened for a few moments to let the herd cross. Then the celebrations began as the beasts danced around the prey, drank a toast to her spilled blood, and led her in a procession to one of the "cemeteries of numbers," where other victims were secretly buried. She would be just another body beneath a numbered metal plate.

The sun was about to set. It dropped behind the sea that raged in memory, bade farewell to the conquered cities, and departed.

ABOUT THE CONTRIBUTORS

Ayman Nobany

OSAMA ALAYSA was born in Bethlehem, Palestine, in 1963. He has worked as a journalist for various Arab and regional newspapers, and has published six novels, four short story collections, and a number of research studies on Palestinian history. His novel *The Fools of Bethlehem* was awarded the Sheikh Zayed Book Award in 2015.

ROGER ALLEN retired in 2011 from the Department of Near Eastern Languages and Civilizations at the University of Pennsylvania. Among his published studies are *The Arabic Novel* and *The Arabic Literary Heritage*. He has translated numerous modern Arab writers, including Egyptian Nobel laureate Naguib Mahfouz, Jabra Ibrahim Jabra, Yusuf Idris, 'Abd al-Rahman Munif, May Telmissany, Bensalem Himmich, Hanan al-Shaykh, and, most recently, Reem Bassiouney.

Bette Chapman

MARILYN BOOTH is the Khalid bin Abdullah Al Saud Professor for the Study of the Contemporary Arab World at Oxford University. Her most recent monograph, *The Career and Communities of Zaynab Fawwaz*, focuses on early feminism, translation, and arabophone women's writing in Egypt and Ottoman Syria. The translator of eighteen books from the Arabic, she was cowinner of the 2019 Man Booker International Prize for her translation of Jokha Alharthi's *Celestial Bodies*.

RAWYA JARJOURA BURBARA was born in Nazareth in 1969. She currently serves as chief inspector director of Arabic at the Ministry of Education, and is a lecturer in Oranim College's language department. Burbara is also a writer, and her tenth book, a collection of short stories titled *I Do Not Want to Get Used to You*, was published in 2021. Her Arabic novel *On the Shores of Wandering* was translated into Hebrew and published by Pardes in 2020.

CATHERINE COBHAM taught Arabic language and literature at the University of St. Andrews until 2022 and has translated the works of many Arab writers, including poetry by Adonis, Mahmoud Darwish, Ghayath Almadhoun, and Tammam Hunaidy, and novels and short stories by Yusuf Idris, Naguib Mahfouz, Hanan al-Shaykh, and Fuad al-Takarli. She has written articles in academic journals, and cowrote with Fabio Caiani *The Iraqi Novel: Key Writers, Key Texts*.

RAPHAEL CORMACK has a PhD in Egyptian theater from the University of Edinburgh. He is an award-winning editor and translator and has written about Arabic culture for the *London Review of Books, Prospect,* and the *Times Literary Supplement,* among others. He is the editor of *The Book of Cairo* and the coeditor of *The Book of Khartoum.*

MAJID ABU GHOSH was born in the village of Amwas in 1959. He is a member of the secretariat of the General Union of Palestinian Writers. He has published numerous works, including *Qalb al-dhi'b* (*The Wolf's Heart*) and *Qitt al-shawari' numur* (*Street Cat Tigers*), the novels *Sara Hamdan* and *'Asl al-malikat* (*Royal Jelly*), and several collections of short stories and poetry.

NUZHA ABU GHOSH was born in Jerusalem in 1954 and holds a degree in education and the Arabic language from al-Quds University. She worked in children's education before concentrating on educational and cultural programs in her hometown community center. Since 2000, she has published two adult novels, one young adult novel, two short story collections, and twenty-three children's books.

SAWAD HUSSAIN is an Arabic translator and litterateur. She was coeditor of the Arabic-English portion of the award-winning Oxford Arabic Dictionary (2014). Her translations have been recognized by English PEN, the Anglo-Omani Society, and the Palestine Book Awards, among others. She holds an MA in modern Arabic literature from SOAS University of London. Her Twitter handle is @sawadhussain.

IBRAHIM JOUHAR is a Palestinian writer born in 1957 in Jabel Mukaber, Jerusalem. He has worked as a lecturer in the Faculty of Arts at al-Quds University, and among his published works are collections of stories for children and adults, cultural and critical studies, and the novel *Ahl al-jabal* (*People of the Mountain*). Along with a number of his colleagues, he was a cofounding member of the Seventh Day Cultural Symposium, launched in Jerusalem in 1991.

NAZIH KASSIS was born in the Palestinian village of Iqrit in 1944, from which he was evacuated to Rama in 1948. He received his BA from the Hebrew University and his PhD from the University of Exeter. Kassis is a lexicographer, translator, researcher, and poet who writes in the spoken Palestinian dialect, and teaches at the Academic Arab College in Haifa. In 2006, he translated *Sadder Than Water*, a collection of selected poems by Samih al-Qassem, from Arabic to English.

ZIAD KHADASH is a Palestinian writer who was born in Jerusalem in 1964. He graduated from Yarmouk University with a BA in Arabic language, and currently lives in Ramallah, where he works as a creative writing teacher. Khadash has published twelve short story collections and participates in many festivals and book fairs throughout the Arab world.

RAFIQA OTHMAN was born in 1959 and is a Palestinian special education teacher, having spent many years working with deaf children. In addition to publishing several pieces of children's literature, she coauthored the book *Three Mothers, Three Daughters: Palestinian Women's Stories*. Since 2019 she has worked at Achva Academic College.

NUZHA AL-RAMLAWI has been a teacher of Arabic language and literature in Jerusalem since 1998. She holds an MA in Arab Islamic history from Birzeit University, and has authored novels, a short story collection, and a children's book. Her latest novel is *Amputated Dreams*.

NANCY ROBERTS is a freelance Arabic-to-English translator and editor who specializes in modern and classical Arabic literature, politics and education, international development, Islamic thought, and interreligious dialogue. Her translations have won the 1994 Arkansas Arabic Translation Award (for Ghada Samman's *Beirut '75*) and the 2018 Sheikh Hamad Award for Translation and International Understanding (for Ibrahim Nasrallah's *Gaza Weddings*). She lives in Wheaton, Illinois.

RAHAF AL-SA'AD grew up in Jerusalem and started writing in high school. She earned a BA in Arabic literature and education, and is currently pursuing an MA in comparative literature from the Hebrew University of Jerusalem. In 2019, she published her first novella, *Layta.*

JAMEEL AL-SALHOUT was born in Jabel Mukaber, Jerusalem. He holds a degree in Arabic literature from Beirut University, and has worked as a schoolteacher and journalist for Palestinian newspapers. In addition to publishing more than fifty books, he has written dozens of articles on literary criticism.

DIMA AL-SAMMAN was born in Jerusalem in 1963. She has published twelve novels, most of them set in Jerusalem, and a story for children. Since 2006 she has been director general of the Jerusalem Affairs Unit of the Palestinian Ministry of Education. She is a board member for a number of cultural and human rights institutions, and is the director and a founding member of the weekly Seventh Day Cultural Symposium, launched in Jerusalem in 1991.

IYAD SHAMASNAH is a Palestinian poet, novelist, and storywriter, born in Jerusalem in 1976. He has published three poetry books and two novels. Additionally, Shamasnah has translated two books from English to Arabic, and has contributed numerous articles, reviews, and literary research papers to magazines and newspapers.

MAHMOUD SHUKAIR was born in Jabal Al-Mukaber, Jerusalem, in 1941. His short stories have been translated into numerous languages, including English, French, Spanish, and Chinese. He was the recipient a Jordanian Writers Association short story award in 1991 and the Mahmoud Darwish Award for Creativity in 2011. He has also been honored by many book festivals, universities, and other cultural institutions.

MUHAMMAD SHURAIM was born in 1962 and writes classic and modern Arabic poetry, as well as short stories and essays. He has published several books of poetry, including *Jawaher alhikmah fi kalila wa Dimna*, which is an adaptation of the seminal Arabic collection of fables, *Kalila wa Dimna*, from prose to poetry.

MAX WEISS is an associate professor of history and Near Eastern studies at Princeton University, where he is also associated faculty in comparative literature. He is the author, most recently, of *Revolutions Aesthetic: A Cultural History of Ba'thist Syria*, and the translator of works by Nihad Sirees, Dunya Mikhail, Mamdouh Azzam, Faysal Khartash, and Alawiya Sobh, among other Arabic writers. He is currently writing an intellectual history of modern Syria.